ECHOES OF ENMITY

STEFANIE CHU

CANARI PUBLISHING

THE PREQUEL TO KNIGHTS OF THE ALLIANCE

ECHOES

OF ENMITY

First Edition: October 2022

ISBN: 978-1-7377125-4-1 (paperback)

Cover by *KC Design Co*

Map by *Janas Art Fantasy Illustration*

Curses are inevitable.

Pray if you must,

but fate offers no sympathy.

The Alliance
of Althaea, Minetta, and Valenia

CANDELA SEA

MORENTA

NARVI

KNIGHTS
ESTATE

SOLI

AGNA

AVON

AKOUN

BAY OF
MINETTA

VENNE

SOLARIN

SAON

MALINO

OBAN

OONA

KESTREL BAY

FAUNA

FALUM

MERSA
TRIBE

TRIBE OF AEGISES

TRIBE OF UMBRAS

VISCARIAN
TRIBE

ALTHACITY

ALTHA
HILLS

ALLETE

ELEGEN

EVALEEN

KISHNIN

ALTHAEAN SEA

EKVELT

NAMANI

RHEA

DESDEMONA

ALTHAEA MAIN

NANAKA

ENDINE

ALTHAEA
MAIN

GANMALI

NAIAD

GULF OF ORIS

OLINA

OPHALLEN

LAKE URABE

TRIBE OF CELTAS

AXILLAIRE

BELLIGMN
TRIBE

XERAN

ALYSSI

ZLAN
TRIBE

TRIBE OF PARAGONS

N

THE HEARTH

W   E

S

THE ALLIANCE

Empire of
ALTHAEA

Councilors
ADDER & SUZAN

ALTHAEA MAIN
Leader: Gaven

AXILLAIRE
Leader: Ahden

EVALEEN
Leader: Landon

ALTHA HILLS
Leader: High Priest

NANAKA
Leader: Yona

OPHALLEN
Leader: Cole

Empire of
MINETTA

Councilors
DAREH & NOVINHA

AVON
Leader: Shiba

SAON
Leader: Ryland

OBAN
Leader: Nivenda

Empire of
VALENIA

Councilors
TAREK & JULIE

Tribe of
PARAGONS

Tribe of
AEGISES

Tribe of
UMBRAS

Tribe of
CELTAS

PROLOGUE

Roselyn was shivering when she came to life. She heard her mother's voice screaming for her to get out of bed. A chilly air brushed against her arms, and she wanted to stay curled up, comfortable in this warm, almost fetal position.

Something rough and thin brushed against the bridge of her nose. It had a refreshing smell, like the dancing waters of the fountain in her family's courtyard, and a dash of the soggy dirt that would accumulate on her pastel-colored shoes.

Was she outside? Roselyn had to open her eyes now.

Nothing.

It was pitch black. She blinked a couple of times to make sure she had not gone blind. Blades of grass tickled her hands and legs, and she knew now where that sensation had come from. Drawn to a cricket's lullaby, she focused on the sounds around her — the staccato of notes filled the still night.

"Joachim?" she called out, breathing heavily. Her voice rang through the darkness, returning to her in echoes of solitude. She wrapped her hands around herself, feeling small and lonely, like a canoe stranded in the Candela Sea.

The world around her began to take shape, and she breathed in relief. But that relief only lasted a moment. She was not in her room, her soft bed nowhere to be seen. Huge, monstrous forms danced in the shadows around her, slow and rocking, darting to the tune of the blowing breeze. They surrounded her, and she saw no end.

Roselyn wanted to cry, but Father said only weak people cry. That couldn't be her. She was a perfect noble, a prodigy admired by every person across the alliance. Besides, she had the protection of the Gods; at least, that was what the heirloom around her neck was for. And her natural, lilac hair — though a much darker shade than her mother's perfect pink — meant she was a favorite among the Gods. They wouldn't let her down now.

Her moist eyes followed the only source of light. It was hovering in the west, meaning it was past midnight. She was thankful she had learned how to tell time by looking at the moon, but she still had no idea where she was.

What good was that information to her?

She sighed, clasping onto the sides of her lacy dress that had blanketed the forest floor. She searched for her pockets. Of course, there were none… but she felt something crunchy. Her eyes darted to the spot — dark and hard like mud had dried there. Only it wasn't mud that ruined her dress; the patch had been burnt.

Even worse, she thought. Mother would be furious.

Then it occurred to her that this was the dress she had worn to her viola performance for the Region Leader in Soli… Was that yesterday? Or maybe the day before. How long had she been sleeping?

It all had to be a dream. Joachim had told her to never be afraid to dream, that dreams had the power to take her places. What he didn't tell her, however, was that she might wind up alone, in the middle of nowhere.

Her body curled in on itself, and she lay still in the cold grass, waiting, hoping Joachim would come to find her soon.

She could feel her nose growing numb in the cold breeze with each passing minute. But the forest was calm; the night was still. Being outside didn't feel like a prison, and the crickets weren't scolding her.

Her mind was slipping into the velvety darkness, eyes closed as she was ferried away into the lands of wishes and imagination. When she woke up again, it'd all be over.

EXCEPT, it wasn't.

Morning birds were chirping noisily in the trees. Their yellow and blue plumages fluttered from branches to nests. The sun was glazing over the horizon; its bright yellow rays pierced the trees and lit up the world.

Roselyn looked around again. She was sitting in the middle of a grass field, surrounded by an endless stretch of oak trees. Her brows furrowed when she realized there was no house in sight, nothing familiar in view. And she still had no idea which direction she came from.

But she had to get home, even if the voice in her told her nothing good awaited her. She picked a direction – out of instinct – and started walking, trudging through the strange land.

Minutes could've passed. Hours? She had no sense of time. Her dry mouth begged like a stray dog, desperate for food, as needles stung her stomach.

The sun was ahead of her when she reached a cluster of berries. They were purple, bright, and looked like the best remedy for her aching stomach. But she recalled the time Joachim warned her that Taurin, the God of Land, sowed fake fruits to tempt and punish misbehaving children. She'd heard stories of wanderers being poisoned by wild berries all the time, so she knew it was true.

She sighed at the cluster of beautiful poison and continued her journey to anywhere.

Her legs felt like logs of wood as she dragged them through the forest one tired step at a time. Branches cracked and splintered, and leaves crushed under her feet. When the sky broke into a burst of golden orange, she realized she hadn't accomplished anything.

Her mind wandered between possible realities. Did walking in an unknown direction make her rescue less probable? What if she never found a way out of here? And most importantly, did she want to be rescued?

The last time she saw her parents, they had been shredding her to pieces with their words. She could still hear their voices stabbing her eardrums; their words would sizzle her like a hot knife on flesh.

Perhaps remaining lost was preferable to the fate that awaited her in the arms of her own parents.

Part of her was relieved. At least she was finally free from her duties and her parents' impossible expectations.

The other part of her wondered if this could really be her destiny – stranded forever in a forest, having accomplished nothing, never to be remembered as anything but a disappointment.

The golden sky made way for the blue of late evening. Cold crept into the forest, and the shadow monsters began gathering in the trees in ambush.

"Joachim..." she whispered, trudging through the nameless forest. Tears blurred her vision. She wiped them with her muddied hands and buried her face in her arms. She didn't want the orange glow of the sun to disappear, but it was fleeing beyond the mountains, her wishes unheard.

"Joachim!" She yelled into the falling night. And like every other time when she called his name, echoes of her voice returned to her, reminding her she was alone in a big, empty world.

She closed her eyes and, with trembling lips, begged to be found.

CHAPTER ONE

"I'm back," Mirari said, stepping into the kitchen. Salathiel had just put out the fire and divided their supper into two plates. She joined her brother at the table, but before she could take a seat, she noticed something was off.

Without looking at her, he let out a big sigh and picked up the fork.

She knew what he was about to say. The sun was gone, and...

"You're late again," Salathiel said.

"Well, today some bum was harassing Miss Raina and—"

"When I ask you to be back by six, I mean it," he said with grave intensity.

Mirari stopped playing around. She sealed her lips shut, letting her gaze drift to the floor. The aroma of rosemary over crispy chicken thighs smelled wonderful, but she didn't feel the least bit hungry anymore.

Mirari tried to defend herself. "Take it easy. Shit happens, alright?"

Salathiel sighed. A familiar look of disappointment washed

over his features. "I can't help it. You're always stirring up trouble."

"The trouble is already there. I just put a stop to it when I can."

"And when you're late, how do I know you weren't knifed in some alley?"

Mirari kept her gaze on the floor. She didn't want to have to justify herself. "I can handle—"

His fist slammed the table. "How many times do I have to tell you to stop getting into brawls?"

She mumbled, "Sorry."

It wasn't the first time they'd got into a quarrel over this, and she knew there was nothing she could say to ease the tension. She kept quiet, letting the tick of the clock and the grinding of his fork against the plate fill the cottage. Her eyes drifted back to Salathiel. His anger was palpable.

He had been like this ever since their home invasion three years ago. Mirari fractured three ribs and was bedridden for two weeks. It would've taken longer had it not been for their talented town healer – gifted with the elemental forces in kore. Salathiel took that incident as a reason to make sure Mirari came home on time, stayed out of trouble, and never got into fights. Yes, Mirari got hurt, but a few broken bones weren't going to stop her from pursuing justice.

While everyone was born with some sort of ability — most being elemental — the power of one's kore was often limited by genetics. Mirari's ancestors were inventors, not fighters, and the art of kore in her bloodline was lost over time. She knew how to play a few tricks with the wind, but that was all. Still, she knew the basics of physical combat as well as Salathiel.

"Sal, you shouldn't worry about me," Mirari said. "You know I can handle them… Besides, it's good sparring practice."

He took a bite and lowered his fork. "If you go looking for trouble, I can guarantee one thing. You'll find it. The less atten-

tion you draw, the better. Whatever happened to laying low…
Roselyn?"

She jerked her head up. He was right. Though they lived in a small trading town in the countryside of Minetta, and she was very comfortable around the people of Solarin, she didn't want rumors to start about a lady merchant who could beat up any drunken bastard.

Still, she persisted. "Someone has to look out for those people."

"But it doesn't have to be you. Sis, I know these street uglies are no match for you, but one bad encounter is all it takes to change the stakes. Besides, how do you think they feel knowing a little girl beat them up?" He picked up her fork, stabbed at a few chunks of carrots, and held the fork in front of her mouth.

"I'm almost nineteen, Sal."

"You're a baby. Eat."

Mirari pouted but accepted the carrots. He let go of the fork while it still dangled in her mouth.

"Be a little selfish for once," he advised. Salathiel's anger had evaporated as soon as the fire was put out. He never stayed mad for long, and Mirari knew he just wanted to be the best brother he could be. "Sticking your nose in other people's business is never a good thing. Trust me, I stopped doing that once I got to know my clients."

"Yeah?" Mirari probed. "And how do you think I feel about your job? You're not the only one who worries."

Salathiel's job was riskier than hers – that he couldn't argue. All she had to do was carry supplies across town. Salathiel had to escort all kinds of shady people around. He was a scrawny young man who looked like he could be dragged off by the wind but could handle knives better than the finest dart players or the most skilled seaside chefs.

"Now, should I be taking orders from my kid sister?"

"We're both adults now."

"Nineteen already, huh?" He reached into his pocket, pulled out a small velvet box, and tossed it at Mirari. She caught it with both her hands and opened the lid just wide enough for her to take a peek inside.

"Early birthday present," Salathiel said with his mouth still full.

Mirari took it by the tip and lifted it out of the box. It was a beautiful bundle of white and gold feathers, secured together with gold gemstones. Her face beamed as brightly as the gemstones.

"I love it. Thank you," Mirari said, securing the pin in her ponytail.

"We found you when you were, what? Six?"

"Mhm. And this month marks ten years since Gaven left."

Salathiel fell silent, almost as if she had angered him again. But she knew he wasn't angry. Salathiel looked like he was trying to hold back a flood of complaints. Hearing Gaven's name always made him uncomfortable, and she couldn't quite understand why. Mirari loved both of them as if they were her real brothers, but Gaven was Salathiel's cousin by blood.

For years, rumors had been circulating about an extraordinary young warrior in Althaea who could take down any Althaean fighter. He hadn't lost a duel in years — remarkable for a man who had walked the earth for barely two decades — and his victories earned him the nickname of the Valiant Tiger. Even region leaders, the most skilled of all fighters and rulers of their respective territories, were afraid to challenge him. Most Minettans saw him as a threat, a new warlord in the making who may have had a thirst for victory beyond Althaean soil.

The fear that Althaea would shatter the alliance and invade Minetta was on everyone's minds. Mirari knew Gaven would never do that, but sometimes she wondered if Salathiel disagreed with her.

"He became a region leader," she said. "That was his dream. We should be proud of him."

"Yeah, a region leader of *Althaea*. Now he's one of those people who blame Minettans for everything. Isn't it ironic? Does it really not bother you that he abandoned everything just to become an Althaean?"

"I thought you supported him."

"I do. It's just..." Salathiel shrugged. "He never wrote to us once. Not a single time in ten years. We did nothing but support him. We took him in when his parents abandoned him, and you helped him make it to Althaea... and he never thanked us for any of that. We're stuck in this shithole while he gets to live in a fancy estate and dine like a king..."

"Sal..." Mirari frowned. "We don't know what he goes through. I'm sure he has his reasons. You know how they treat Minettans over there. If anyone found a connection between him and us, we'd all be in grave danger. We can only hope that one day he'll come back to us... when he's ready."

Salathiel took a deep breath. "If that's what you want to believe." He took one last bite before putting his plate in the sink. "But until then, I have no choice but to assume he wants nothing to do with us anymore."

It was jealous rage, she knew. All of Salathiel's life, Gaven always got what he wanted and never had to work for it. Meanwhile, Salathiel kept working as if he didn't do enough for his family, always wanting to do better, work harder, provide more, take on bigger jobs. It was the only thing he could do, he once told her, for in this cruel world a peasant was forever a peasant... unless you got lucky like Gaven.

Salathiel grabbed his coat by the door and ran his fingers through his hair in the small fogged mirror hanging by the coat rack.

"You have a job tonight?" Mirari thought they were going to spend the evening together.

"Yeah. The one I told you about."

Her eyes widened.

Earlier that week, he had been offered an unbelievable sum of money to guard a meeting with some important officials in town. The details of the meeting were a secret, of course, but it paid tenfold the amount Salathiel would make in one night.

"Sal! I thought you said you weren't going to take it."

"We could really use that money to fix the foundation," Salathiel said, gesturing to the squeaky wooden planks on the floor. "Or maybe build a new one altogether."

Mirari didn't argue with that, but a refurbished home was a luxury that she was content living without. She would much rather have him safe. But unlike Salathiel, Mirari was the younger sibling, and she knew she could do little to stop him.

"Please be careful. What time?"

"I want to say midnight, but if I'm not back by two, you have permission to come look for me... and if the roof starts leaking again, use the chicken pot in the sink."

Salathiel walked back over to the table and hugged her.

"I want to paint the roof blue," Mirari said.

"Deal. And we'll use the rest of the money to celebrate your actual birthday."

"No!" Mirari blurted. "Don't say that. It's bad luck."

Salathiel chuckled as he waved her one last goodbye before he left.

CHAPTER TWO

Mirari couldn't sleep that night. She tossed and turned, wide awake in her bed, listening to water slowly dripping into the chicken pot. She turned over and looked at the clock. Nearly one.

Salathiel rarely stayed out this late and never overnight. She predicted he would be back any minute now.

Mirari shut her eyes again, meditating over the pitter-patter. Ten past one.

What would she do if he was not back by two? He said she could then go out looking for him, but he was kidding... wasn't he?

The dripping water was no longer peaceful but rather a reminder of every second that passed. She threw the blanket over her head and shut her eyes.

She told herself not to think about it. But she couldn't ignore the gut feeling that something wasn't right.

She pushed herself out of bed and peeked into the room next to hers. The door was still open. Everything was untouched in the living room. The front door only had a single pair of shoes next to it – hers.

With every tick of the clock, she hoped he would come through that door. It kept ticking. Her mind ricocheted from one stupid thing to the next.

Maybe the client insisted he go out drinking with them.

Could have gotten food poisoning, and he's puking his guts out.

Perhaps he twisted his ankle and couldn't walk up the hill.

She was desperate to believe it, to believe anything except the terror that was clawing at her heart.

She had made up her mind. If Salathiel didn't return in three minutes, she would go look for him. She wanted so badly to hear the jingle of his keys, the turn of the lock...

She watched as the clock went past its mark. She was having second thoughts about leaving. What if he came back and she was gone? He'd be furious. She could leave him a note. Tomorrow they'd laugh about how paranoid she was being, but...

Something told her Salathiel was in danger. Mirari snatched her coat from the peg and pulled the front door open. A gust of fresh air brushed against her face and weaved through her hair. She closed the door behind her, welcoming the cold and dark night. The fireflies were resting under the bright moon that illuminated the hills around Solarin. She scanned the entire plain, but there was no one. She strode down the road Salathiel always took when he went to work.

She arrived at the ramshackle security agency. As expected, Mirari could see a dim light flicker from inside the shack. A young man was half asleep with his head balanced on his arm. He sprang awake as soon as he heard Mirari's knock. He sat up and leaned out the window.

"Has Salathiel Zanette returned from his job tonight?" Mirari asked.

The man tipped back to glance at his small clock on the

table. He then sifted through a small stack of papers at his desk and ran down a table of names until he found the one.

"He didn't check out tonight… but his client has left."

"What does that mean?"

"They left town. They were from—" He stopped himself. "… out of town. That's all I know."

"Then shouldn't Sal be back too?"

"Maybe he forgot to sign out before going home."

"He's not at home. That's why I'm here."

The man yawned loudly, stretching his mouth as wide as possible. He blinked a few times to push his tired tears out of the way and shook his head.

"Well… I'm sorry, Miss. I'm just as clueless as you are. You can talk to the boss tomorrow."

Mirari turned away. She had no other choice.

She wandered around town for as long as the moonlight guided her way. She saw nothing but open fields and sleeping cattle. Not even the few houses she passed by had any candles lit. Normally she enjoyed the still night, but tonight was unsettling. She stopped at the edge of the forest, wondering if, for any reason, he would've been in there. Leaves shuffling above her set a haunting tone. It reminded her of the time she woke up in the forest alone. The memories of unknown creatures hiding in thick shrubs and stretches of trees that would go on endlessly triggered the fear of being lost again.

But she swallowed that fear and stepped into the dark void — she owed this much to Salathiel and Gaven. They rescued her, and she would do the same for them in a heartbeat.

She called his name, heedless of the potential creatures drawn to her voice. She paid no attention to the uneven surface beneath her feet as she pushed forward.

She called for him again and again until the sounds of nature started to return. Flocks of jays and robins flew overhead, and a few rabbits crossed her path. But while nature welcomed the new day, Mirari was still living in a nightmare. She ignored the pain in her feet and carried on, lying to herself that he would be found.

CHAPTER THREE

The streets of Althaea Main were bustling with merchants and workers. The famished sat along the musky cobblestone roads, glaring at Althaean soldiers – vermin in chainmail. Under a dark cloud of smog, it would be another day of abuse from unregulated factory owners and land barons who submerged their workers in long hours of labor. Enduring these conditions was better than giving region leaders a reason to raise taxes, which placed burdens heavier than the stones excavated from the mines. Althaeans took home what they could and prayed it would be enough to survive the night.

As much as Althaeans didn't want to admit it, they needed foreigners to bring in new opportunities and imports to feed malnourished workers. The empire was abundant in raw minerals, but what good were they if they were limited to the craftmanship of second-rate Althaean inventors? Althaea could not reach its full potential without help from other empires – it was an unpopular opinion but one Region Leader Gaven had always believed in.

He stood cross-armed in the shaded war room, watching Councilor Suzan arrange metal figurines over a map of Althaea.

The map was brought to life with particles of hāstal, crafting a geometric replica of the landscape using an oriōn. Such devices were constructed by the greatest inventors of the Hale family, who discovered that raw crystal energy could be fused with kore to create new technology. Suddenly, victory was no longer dependent on the fighter and the kore affinity they were born with, but also how many hāstal inventions they had at their disposal.

Suzan dropped each figurine, creating a glow on the map. A large cluster was concentrated over a center region labeled 'Althaea Main'. Gaven could see why she was displeased.

"Do we have a problem, *Your Grace*?" Gaven said.

"Abolishing the Separation Law? Have you gone mad?" she said. She raised her cane over the table, tapping over the capital. "This is career suicide. What did I tell you about making impulsive decisions during the first couple of years?"

Althaeans were used to foreigners traveling in their empire, but those people came only on official business. A Minettan, Valenian, or any other person of a different origin was forbidden to plant their roots on Althaean soil. That was the way the law was set since the formation of the Council hundreds of years ago. Over the last century, Minetta and Valenia began abolishing the Separation Law in their regions. Co-existence was the norm in those territories, but Althaea stayed frozen in time, until now.

From the corner of his eye, Gaven could see Erel's intimidating glare. Her brown cowl covered most of her face – but not those golden eyes. She and Commander Haynes huddled against a wall, their hands respectfully behind their backs and chins raised high, more for the benefit of Councilor Suzan than for their region leader.

Gaven recalled Erel giving him the same stern warning back when talk of a rebellion was limited to a drunk man's nonsense. Erel spent decades on the streets, forced to listen to preposterous ideologies from disgruntled commoners. She knew what the

18

people wanted and how they viewed Gaven. But he didn't always listen to his second in command.

Gaven turned his attention back to Suzan, insisting. "You wanted Althaea to be progressive. It's time we stop blaming the other empires for our fallout and work with them to prosper an actual alliance."

"Riots are growing everywhere," Suzan said. "They started from here after what you did."

"I'm only doing what you were afraid to do for decades."

Erel and Haynes turned white. No one would dare speak to a legendary fighter like that, especially one currently sitting at a seat on the Council. Much like Gaven when he was a trainee, Suzan earned her respect through her army's ranks the way all Althaeans did – through duels. Gaven knew she could humiliate all of them in combat without drawing a weapon, a reputation that she maintained to this day on the battlefield and in court. But Suzan was like the mother Gaven never had. He respected her, but he wasn't afraid.

Suzan let out a hefty sigh and shook her head. "If you can't control your people, no one will take you seriously. It's as simple as that. Take care of these rebels before it gets out of hand."

Silencing was the Althaean way to handle all issues. But what if he could change that? Show that it was possible to communicate with words before the sword?

Gaven saw the riots differently. It wasn't about the Althaean reluctance to live among Minettans and Valenians. He had seen the unrest and dissatisfaction festering for months, years in fact, even when Suzan was in power. Disdain was fueled by decades of frustration for the common man who had no say in anything the ruling class did. Many had given up the fight, accepting hardship as the norm, but revoking the Separation Law gave an excuse for the extremists to start trouble.

Suzan came with a message from the Council, and her demands were non-negotiable. It was an unfortunate case where they would need to show brute force to calm the people. They wanted to make an example of these radicals.

"Sometimes silencing *is* the way to peace. Learn to take defeat." She turned her head to the wall. "Lady Erel, don't you agree?"

Erel lowered her head and said, "We'll start with the eastern region, go with the same ring strategy we used in Desdemona. Haynes will surround the city with troops." Haynes responded with a firm nod. It was an efficient plan… if all one wanted to accomplish was a slaughter.

"Very good. Gaven, try to listen to your teammates for once."

Suzan reached for her white coat on a nearby stool and secured it over her body before heading for the door. As soon as he heard the door lock behind her, Gaven bristled at his commanders.

Haynes raised his hands, cowering behind them. "Sorry, My Lord. Between you and Councilor Suzan, she always has the last say."

"She's right," Erel said, walking over to the table and pointing at the map. "If the rebellion has spread this much, the time for talk is behind us. If you want to keep your place as region leader, if you want this empire to stand tomorrow, you must overthrow them before they overthrow you."

Perhaps there was truth to Erel's words. Over the last few years, Gaven had been confident he was making the right decisions. But despite all he could do to uphold justice, reform the bureaucracy, and give citizens more of a voice, Gaven found all his efforts to improve the lives of his people to be futile.

There was a loud knock on the door, which Erel answered before Gaven had a chance to look up.

"No interruptions!" She hissed at the young soldier decorated in steel. She was taken aback, nose crinkling, when she noticed his armor was stained in an assortment of green and brown sludge and a fresh cut on his cheek.

"A-apologies, Milady," the soldier bowed. "They broke through the first gate. The infirmary is being overwhelmed. We need orders now, Your Honor."

Erel turned to Gaven, who had his gaze fixed on the map. It wouldn't be the first time he had to resort to violence with his people, but it didn't make the feeling any less painful.

His hand lingered toward a compact weapon resting on the edge of the table, one that could've been mistaken for an official scroll sent by the Council. His fingers admired its sheath before snatching it and tossing it toward the door. It fell perfectly in the soldier's hands. He unlocked the weapon, and with a click, the stick expanded into a spear with blades rising from both ends. Purple sparks danced around the blades, fully charged and ready to asphyxiate anyone within its reach.

"Leave no one alive."

CHAPTER FOUR

W eeks passed without any news of Salathiel. Mirari had tried everything she could to follow his trail, to find some clue. But the information was drier than the deserts of Axillaire, and no one was willing to help her. Days passed slowly as she spent hours on end lying on the rough couch in their cottage, hoping he would come through the door. She no longer had an interest in the two history books she had nearly finished. Instead, she found peace in staring at the dusty countertops she hadn't cleaned for weeks and the fireplace she didn't care to light anymore. When it rained, she threw the bucket where the roof leaked and immersed herself in the pitter-patter. But even though the dripping eventually stopped, and the sun's rays shone through their skylight once more, time felt as if it was forever frozen.

The whole town knew about Salathiel's disappearance at this point. Mirari asked everyone, but most simply dismissed it as another unfortunate encounter with fate. It was not uncommon in the countryside, and unless you were a noble, no one cared.

She ate stale bread if she had the appetite to eat at all. She didn't dare leave the cottage to get more food — Salathiel could come home any minute.

Mirari was lying on the sofa, playing with one of Salathiel's daggers, when there was a knock on the door, then she heard a familiar deep voice. It was old and husky but still carried the same gentle whisper that used to caress her to sleep whenever her parents got into a fight.

"Miss?" he said. "I know you're in there, child. Please, open the—"

She sprung to her feet and flung the door open. It wasn't Salathiel, but the old, scarred man was the closest thing to a family she had left. She threw herself into Joachim's arms, weeping her heart out. She could feel the daggers hidden inside his gold-trimmed, brown coat. He never changed, and it made her feel safe.

He just held her, letting her cry, rocking her gently, patting her back, and telling her it would be all right.

Joachim took her inside, sat her on the couch, and bustled around making tea.

"Walk me through it," he said. "Let's retrace your steps."

Mirari told him everything she knew about Salathiel's disappearance, detailing the people she asked and the areas she checked. Joachim nodded as he sipped his tea. He had a concerned look, which told Mirari she already knew the answer. Still, he offered his expertise, if not some closure.

He wasn't obligated to assist her. Mirari had long severed her connection with the Hale family, along with her birth name, when she ran away from home. When he found her in the safe hands of Salathiel, it was clear why she didn't want to return, and he respected her decision. His loyalty wasn't to the Hale family but rather to Roselyn. He would serve as her retainer until death.

Joachim stared into his now empty cup, then said, "He should've listened to you, but what's done is done." He stood up and picked up his coat. "Come, now. We need to find out more about these clients."

Mirari returned to the office of Salathiel's employer – this time with Joachim behind her. She entered the tiny wooden shack. It was big enough to fit ten people, but there was only one desk and only one person inside at all times. Mirari ignored the two rough-looking guards that stood next to the door. They gave her a nasty glare but didn't dare to touch her, wary of the array of daggers on Joachim's belt.

She saw the lazy boss with a beer belly. It could've been mistaken as an eight-month pregnancy if he did not have a halo for his hair and a year-old unmanaged beard.

"You again?" He scoffed as Mirari shut the door. "I already told you. I have no idea where your brother is. For all I know, he could be slacking on the job."

Mirari fumed with no restraint. "Do you think Sal is that kind of person?"

"Either that or he got killed on the job. Whichever, not my problem."

Her anger collected in her fist. "Maybe I should make it your problem."

Joachim restrained her from getting any closer to the boss and gave her that steady glare she had become accustomed to reading as a child.

"What organization was he guarding?" Joachim asked.

"It's confidential."

"Do you want to talk to her or me?" Joachim gestured to Mirari, and she pounded her fists together a few times.

"Hey, I ju… I don't want to get involved. I take my clients' confidentiality very seriously. I wouldn't be in business long if I told you."

Mirari approached again, menacing. "You won't be in business in five minutes if you don't tell me."

Joachim put a hand on her shoulder and said, "Please. That's not necessary."

The employer raised his hands in an attempt to shield his disheveled face. Sweat was beginning to collect on his brow. "I told you. These guys were in town for a few days, and they specifically requested Salathiel to guard them during their meeting. That's all I can say."

That caught Joachim's attention. Salathiel was explicitly targeted by whoever hired him.

Cracking her knuckles, Mirari stepped around Joachim. "We're not getting anywhere like this."

The man blanched. "Now, you just... you both best be getting out of here before I call in my boys. I'm still cleaning up the mess you left last time." The man pointed to the broken cabinet in the corner of the room. Under it was a scattering of papers he hadn't bothered to pick up.

Mirari swiped her hand to the side, and an aggressive gust followed. In the compact office, the papers on his desk circled in a mini-tornado before scattering across the floor.

Hearing the commotion, the two guards rushed into the room. They looked at the blizzard of papers on the floor.

"What do you think you're doing?" demanded the bigger guard. He lunged forward, but Joachim kicked his foot out, causing the man to fall back against the wall.

"Jogging his memory," Mirari answered, tingling the few sparks of kore in her palm. She swiped her hand again, the wind throwing the broken cabinet at them while they were distracted. The cabinet hit the last man standing in the head, instantly rendering him unconscious and plowing him into the other fallen guard. The boss flinched, seeing his guards were taken out in seconds. Mirari slammed her hands on the table in front of him.

"Tell me about these men!"

"Hey, hey, hey," the boss said. "I'm honest, sweetheart. If I tell you who they were, they'll come back and kill all of us. That amount of money comes at a price."

"Where did they meet?" Joachim asked.

"Like I said, confid—" He let out a squeal sharper than a poppy fox in a bear trap. Joachim had him by the ear, ignoring the man's pleas. "D-do you know the place they call 'Smugglers' Dell'?"

"But... I already searched there," Mirari said.

Joachim released his grip, and the boss sighed a relief. He stayed on the ground, saying, "And I guarantee you still won't find anything. Now leave before you get us all in trouble."

IT WAS a small clearing in the forest, marked only by a niche created by the overhang of two rocks. Mirari and Joachim searched in bushes, under rocks, and even in the cover of pine needles. Mirari wasn't expecting much, having scoured the place herself, but Joachim picked up on something she wasn't strong enough to detect – someone's aura.

"Spells were used here," Joachim said. His eyes crinkled in an uneasy way that puzzled Mirari.

"How do you know?"

"The energy here is still high. This may be..."

"May be what?"

"It feels like a dark aura."

"Dark aura? There's such a thing?"

"A person's spiritual energy is known as light aura, but we've always referred to it as simply aura. Mainly because dark aura is extremely rare, and in modern times, people simply dismiss its existence."

"What's the difference?"

"Dark aura is much stronger. The people with it, well, we

consider it a curse. People aren't born with a dark aura. Their numbers… maybe less than ten in the whole world."

"What does that mean?"

"No one knows. And it's not something you'd want to find out, Lady Mirari."

Joachim took one last look at the empty area around them, then took Mirari by the arm and escorted her out of the forest.

"What's the rush?"

"This is a cursed place."

Mirari planted her feet and pulled away. "What's the matter with you?"

"Come along now. Please." He reached for her again, but she dodged away.

"Not until I get some answers. This isn't like you, Joachim. What are you so scared of?"

Joachim's eyes swept all around them, even scanning the tree branches above. "Lady Mirari, I believe it's in your best interest that you leave this behind you."

"What do you mean? You're giving up on finding Sal?"

"*We* are giving up," he corrected.

"Joachim, if there is something you're not telling me, I demand you to inform me."

"Not here."

"Why? There's nobody here."

"No one we can see. But there are protective wards. They will know we were here."

"Who will?"

"Please, come now. It's getting dark."

When they finally emerged out of the forest, the sun was setting, and the twilight was growing dim. They could see the lights in town begin to wink out, one by one.

Mirari stopped again, patience running thin. "Is this good enough? Or do we have to hide under the bed before you talk?"

Joachim sighed. Then, reluctantly, he began. "Sal had mentioned to me that you pick fights in town."

"I don't pick fights," Mirari said. "I stop the ones already happening."

"You're sticking your nose in other people's business, Lady Mirari," Joachim warned. "It's unwise."

"Why are you ducking the question? What is it that you're so scared of that we should quit searching for him?"

"Why do you go looking for trouble?"

"I'm just helping people who can't defend themselves. What's wrong with that?"

"I would never ask you to change your kind nature, Lady Mirari. But just because I taught you how to fight doesn't mean that you should. You make enemies that way."

"So you'd rather let people tyrannize each other?"

"It is the world we live in, and it cannot be changed."

"I say otherwise."

"And *I* say this with all seriousness, Lady Mirari. Do not involve yourself in these petty fights again."

Mirari held her tongue. She could tell Joachim really meant it this time, and she was disturbed that he was upset with her. "You tell me why you're so jumpy all of a sudden, and I'll think about it. Okay?"

Joachim was quiet for a long time. She couldn't take it. "Joachim? Hello?"

He didn't look at her, but hushed words began to fall from his lips. It looked like each one tore out a piece of him. "There is an organization that has gathered... attention over the past few years. It is said they are called 'the Blessed'." Joachim paused, trying to swallow, his throat filled with sand. "Rumor has it that some of its members possess dark aura. After what we saw — what I felt — in those woods... I fear it is more than gossip. It may be true."

"And you think these 'Blessed' jokers took Sal?"

"I don't know. Many will tell you the organization is a myth. Those who know it's not will tell you the same. If you ever encounter someone from the Blessed, well… you don't speak of it, not if you want to live. That's why Salathiel's employer didn't want to say anything."

"How do you know if someone is a part of the Blessed?"

"You don't. It looks like Sal got the bad end of it."

"Are you saying that he…" Mirari couldn't finish her sentence.

"Lady Mirari, we have to assume he's not with us anymore."

"But what if he's alive? We won't know until we find him."

"There's nothing we can do. I'm sorry, Lady Mirari."

Death had crossed her mind before, but she didn't expect to hear it out loud, not from Joachim. There was no way he was gone. In her heart, she knew Salathiel was still alive and out there somewhere. He had to be.

She was too shocked to cry. Mirari kept telling herself Salathiel would show up soon. And she couldn't help but wonder, what did the Blessed want with him?

CHAPTER FIVE

E rel kept her eyes on the projected map, her finger pointed at the landscape of a village in the North. They were huddled in the back room of the keep, shaded by tacky sapphire curtains — likely from five generations ago. The far end of the table, where Haynes had rested his head, was littered with crumbs from this morning's bread. Erel avoided that area, wanting to spare her toes from the minefield of unknown objects. The room had been unkept for weeks and would remain so for as long as the riots continued.

A soft glow illuminated Gaven's face as he stared over several metal figurines on the map. His army cracked down several riots throughout Althaea Main. The plan was working, but how many more mass murders did he have to commit until the riots ended? Until the Council was satisfied?

"Are we done yet?" Haynes whined as he stretched his stiff legs. The three had been working since dawn, feet sore and mouths parched from hours of discussion. Day after day, it was all the same. Compared to the armies suppressing their rebellion, the commoners didn't have the resources or fighting skill sets to win. But they had willpower, and that was what made this uprising particularly troublesome.

The city of Rhea was next. The rioters there had burned the local garrison, taken over the city granaries, looted a temple, and occupied city hall. The Earl of Rhea fled for his life, and his estate was sacked and burned.

Erel slapped Haynes' bottom with her long wooden pointer. "We still haven't talked about the supply allocation. You only get two shield tanks this time."

"Two?" Haynes slammed his hands on the table and wailed like a child. "Last time it was four."

"That was before you broke one."

"That was an accident. Tell her it was an accident, My Lord."

Gaven didn't seem to care. His head was turned to the door, distracted by a knock.

Erel had ignored it, much like she had ignored every disturbance that day. But the knocks did not stop. They were frantic and unwelcoming. Gaven rose from his seat — perhaps out of boredom — and stepped out into the next room, a waiting area that he had remodeled into a reading nook. It contained walls of bookshelves, a few velvet couches, exotic rugs from Axillaire, and the door to the hallway. The person on the other side of the door was about to get a scolding, no doubt. Erel left him to it.

"Rain has been reported in this area over the past few days," Erel said, sweeping her pointer over to the hillside. "It may give some of the rebels an escape path, but it's better than dragging our horses through the mud." She noticed Haynes's focus was elsewhere, lining the extra figurines on a blank corner of the map. Erel groaned, dropped her pointer, and sunk into her chair. "Are you even listening?"

"No need to get worked up," Haynes said as he lined up another figurine. "We've done this a dozen times, and it always works. Besides, at this point, those peasants probably don't have much morale left. You know what we should do? There's an amazing alehouse just a few blocks from the eastern gate..."

Erel decided to wait for Gaven, turning out of Haynes' nonsense. She was hearing bits of Gaven's conversation with the person at the door. Something about people dying... and stopping the raids. Gaven was arguing back.

Thud.

Erel turned her head to the curtains that led to the next room. Perhaps it was her imagination, as Haynes didn't react in the slightest. He was still going on about the alehouse, drowning Erel's ability to hear the conversation in the other room.

They heard Gaven scream.

They jumped to their feet. Haynes reached for a sword propped on the wall, but Erel held her finger to her lips, her other hand over the sword, prompting him to let go.

She shook her head and whispered, "I'll check. Call the guards."

Haynes peeked under a pile of cups and papers, then searched another pile. He should've had his clōve on at all times, but the scatterbrain didn't think the communication gloves were necessary within fortress walls. He searched frantically for the pair of black gloves, hoping its soft illuminating threads would stand out in the dark room.

Meanwhile, Erel hugged the walls like a vigilant snake, slipping through the entrance without wavering the curtains.

In the small library, a man had wrestled Gaven to the ground. He appeared distraught, too focused on Gaven to notice Erel slithering from behind. He was a thin man with a faint scar over his left eye, dressed in a simple white shirt and dark pants, unlike any assassin Erel had seen before.

But it wasn't his appearance that troubled Erel. She analyzed every detail of the man, from the pigments on his skin to the frame of his body. Then she listened to his breath, found every vein that coursed to his heart, and listened.

...But there was nothing. This man had no aura, no heartbeat to follow. She didn't know what to make of it.

She turned to Gaven. Her face drained to white when she noticed an eerie mist coiled around his body. The light in his eyes went dull as death as he started to drift into a numb slumber.

The man brushed himself off the ground and headed for the door. He skidded to a stop when a figure blocked his way. Before him was the impossible – the Valiant Tiger, a mere breath away with a glare that could kill.

"Gaven... How did you..."

"Who are you?"

The man turned back to check if he was delusional. Sure enough, the region leader was still on the floor, now sedated. As he turned back, the man reached for the daggers in his belt, but before he could pull one out, the apparition was gone.

He felt something tackle his abdomen and noticed a petite lady had replaced the fake 'Gaven'. She shoved him into a bookshelf, grappling as they went down. As novels and textbooks struck their heads, Erel snatched the daggers from his belt and lodged the weapons into their owner.

He snarled, feeling those blades dig deep into his shoulder and chest. Erel pushed herself up, sinking the weapons deeper into the intruder's chest.

Her eyes were drawn to the strange wounds. A black liquid oozed out like oil. Her brows furrowed in confusion and disgust.

She stared at it for far too long. With his free hand, the man grabbed Erel's left wrist and squeezed it tightly. She tugged and punched, but the man didn't let go. The mist returned like a plague, and Erel's face went pale.

She leaned forward and sunk her teeth deep into his hand. What was it? Would it be poisonous? She didn't care. The man grunted and yanked his hand back, readied it into a fist, then launched forward again.

She tumbled to the side, cheek in pain, but her focus was on the tingling sensation on her hand. She shook her hand, hoping the haze would dissipate, but it was imprinted on her body. She could do nothing but watch as it wrapped around her, and she felt her body grow heavy.

She struggled to catch a breath. The room began to tilt and turn gray, all but the pool of blood seeping from the furniture. Then she heard a soft voice calling her name. She had seen this before and knew where it was headed.

"Haynes!" she yelled. She screamed and hissed at herself, clawing at her arms to shake off the uncanny feeling.

The warrior dashed into the room, but it was too late. He examined the dark phenomenon on Erel and reached out to touch it. She hissed at him, as intimidating as a six-fanged snake. He retracted quickly.

Erel took deep breaths, ignoring the whispers in her mind, her vision slowly coming back into focus. She could now make out the blond commander standing where the shadows were just a second ago. Color had returned to the room — the rainbow of leather-bound books, mahogany tables, and sapphire curtains. The blood was gone... and so was the perpetrator.

"Get... him..." Erel said.

"But..."

Erel nudged him. "I said go..."

Haynes stumbled for the door, tripping over himself only once, in pursuit of the intruder.

Erel took a deep breath and rested against the cedarwood floor. The mist started to fade, melting into the ground. Her head still throbbed, and her limbs quivered as if she hadn't moved for weeks. She turned to her lord, who didn't seem to have the same luck.

"Your Honor?" Erel called out. "This is no time for a nap."

The mist surrounding him had also disappeared, but his eyes stayed shut. She shook him again with her frail hand. His body wobbled like a drunk bum, but he remained still.

"By the Gods," Erel cursed as she pulled together the last of her strength to carry her leader over her back into his private chambers.

CHAPTER SIX

A gentle wind played with the foliage on the cold ground. With every step she took, her bare feet smashed the long-dead leaves. It felt insulting – disturbing things that had already died. But how could she avoid it? As far as her eyes could see through a curtain of smoke, there wasn't an inch of ground bare of orange, red, and brown.

Through her blurred vision, she thought she saw her best friend. No face, but she knew that physique better than anyone. Erel didn't care where she was or why the trees were gray. She hadn't seen this girl in decades… and she hadn't aged a day.

A dozen more figures began to emerge from all directions. When they got close enough, she saw her parents and her siblings. Their faces remained obscured, but they all had the same sleek hair — ranging in color from honeydew to lime — and golden eyes like her.

Her vision began to mold. The figures transformed into dark silhouettes with bloodshot eyes. Gashes covered their bodies and opened a waterfall of blood down their arms. The harrowing cries of her young siblings filled her ears.

Why did you leave, Erel?

Why didn't you come back for us?

How could you have run off?

Erel screamed, begging for it to stop. She reached out with her heavy hand, trying to claw at the tiny shadows. She wanted to strangle them, kill them.

You... do not get to judge me. You... do not control me!

She grasped onto those shadows, yanking them apart. She clawed and pulled at every last one of them. When she got to the girl's shadow, she had to step back. The shadow grinned at her condescendingly. That was how Erel knew it couldn't be her friend.

You let me die, you coward!

The shadow hissed at Erel, reaching for her throat. But before she could grasp her, Erel reached out. She grabbed the shadow by the neck, strangling her best friend.

"If I could go back and save everyone, I would," Erel said, with a tear ready to fall down her cheek. "But I can't change the past. You will never come back. All I can do now... is what you told me to do... to live!"

Erel stretched the shadow harder until the body split open, and a white light emerged from the center, growing brighter and brighter. The light chased away the shadows, and red tainted the room... Everything disappeared.

Erel gasped as her eyes shot wide open. She placed her hand over her mouth, beckoning herself to stay calm. In the dark, she recognized the ornate ceilings and tacky beads that hung along the curtain. She sprung to her feet, brushing back her long hair and shifting into the short woman they all knew her as. She had always admired her companion's cedarwood hair more, but Erel was putting on more than just a fake identity. She was carrying courage.

She dashed out of her room and down the hall, brushing away the guards in front of Gaven's chambers. When she entered, she was surprised to see that he was still awake.

Gaven had woken up not long after he was placed in his chambers, and she'd debriefed him on the attack. Erel made sure the healers did a thorough check, but he seemed normal, as energetic as a servant on her first day. Still, she forced him to get bed rest. They were still looking for the man responsible for his assault, but Gaven didn't care and even told them to disregard it and pretend it never happened. It would be a secret between the three of them.

Now he sat on the edge of his bed, with nothing but the moonlight brightening the room. He sat still, staring at the wall. Erel sighed when she saw that his sheets were tucked, the same as she left them.

"Have you gone daft?" she said. "What are you staring at?"

Without taking his eyes off the wall, he replied with a monotone voice. "I like the silence."

"You need rest. If not, I'll get the healer—"

"No. I am fine."

Erel furrowed her brow. She walked up to his side and took a seat on the cold, marble floor.

"He attacked me too," she said with a tender voice she had never projected before. "They're not real, Your Honor. Whatever you saw—"

"Are the preparations complete?"

Her jaw dropped. "Your Honor, you can't still be thinking about the raid today. You're in no condition to fight."

His face remained blank, now fixated on the moonlight on the balcony beyond the glass doors, looking out to the courtyard.

"We can't have the soldiers worrying over nothing," Gaven said. "The raid goes on."

Gaven was ignoring his health again, putting his honor and duty above all else, and Erel knew there was little she could do to stop her ambitious leader. Still, the events left an uneasy feeling in her stomach. She had no idea what the man wanted or what kind of power he possessed. Gaven seemed to have known him

— he wouldn't have had such an animated discussion with a stranger — but he couldn't recall his face. Were the effects of that dark mist still clouding his memory, or was he trying to protect the man?

Erel rubbed her eyes, still feeling nauseous from the nightmares and hallucinations. She may have underestimated her leader, who overcame the effects of the dark mist faster than she did. She stretched her arms and stood up, waving at him as she walked toward the door. "Three hours until sunrise. You're not going anywhere if you don't get some sleep."

RHEA SAT in a valley flanked by a river to its east and north and two large ridges on the west and south. Haynes peered down the slope at the town, shrouded in a cool morning mist, slightly obscuring the town from view. He had taken the western ridge along with his men, and Erel was moving to the southern ridge. She would pinch the rebel forces from behind as Haynes charged from the side. He took a breath of the cold air and looked down the row of cavalry to either side.

The morning air brought steam across the line of horses. Their blood was still pumping from the ride, stomping and whinnying in anticipation; they looked ominous in the clouds of hot breath that wreathed their manes. The men and women astride their mounts were just as anxious, fidgeting in their seats as the first ray of sunrise broke the morning clouds. It rained on the ride to their positions, and the mud was slick, giving off a swampy smell that turned Haynes' nose.

He looked at the slope overlooking the town from the south and could see Erel and her cavalry reaching their position. Erel had taken command of half of Gaven's forces while Haynes took the other.

He turned back toward the plateau behind him, where the

remaining reserve foot soldiers were staged and ready to follow the cavalry if needed. Still, he could not see the Valiant Tiger's familiar form moving with the troops.

It was unusual for the leader to disappear like this. Haynes had sent his own guards to search for him, but he had yet to hear any good news.

Gaven was due at Rhea along with Haynes and Erel, but he wasn't answering his clōve. The hāstal-sewn communication device should have been able to reach him. Haynes had to use all the military bearing trained in him to not look panicked. He tapped on the black glove — its blue fluorescent threads illuminated and pulsed — and called Erel instead.

"Are you sure he left his chambers this morning?" Haynes asked.

"Before the break of dawn, along with his horse," Erel confirmed. "I didn't expect him to be taking more than a morning stroll."

"I don't recommend holding out any longer," Haynes said. He took notice that his men were wandering around, growing impatient. "You're in charge now, Erel. What's the plan? Do we go look for him or go without him?"

Erel took a look at the foot soldiers she was in command of. They were starting to mutter to each other, spreading rumors that questioned the plan, wondering if it was ill-planned, and doubting this mission's success rate.

"He wouldn't back out," Erel said. "Count to ten, then start moving in."

Haynes had a look of certainty on his face. He spoke to the trooper holding the bugle with a calm, strong voice. "Sound the order, boy. We're moving out!"

Haynes lifted his arm, flagged for the bugle to advance, and moved with his men as they descended the slope.

The village was quiet in the early morning, lazy smoke

drifting from chimneys. A soft glow of sunrise fell on his face, and the mist cleared as they got closer.

To his amazement, the village appeared to have little in the way of defense. Excitement climbed his spine as he called out, "Their defenses are half built. We will rout this rabble in no time." Haynes leveled his sword, and his horse began to gallop as the force moved in unison. "Call for the southern flank!"

A bugle sounded behind him, and he saw dark shapes appear along the ridge to their right. Erel's cavalry poured over the edge of the ridge and descended upon the town as Haynes entered the empty streets, sword ready to strike anyone in his way.

The men and horses charged in, yet the streets and buildings were quiet. Haynes led the column through the main road and into the town square, careful not to rush his horse through the slick muddy streets. As they entered the square, Haynes found Erel and her forces entering from the other side.

"Where in Inferna are they?" she said, and Haynes looked at the homes.

"Clear the houses."

A handful of men dismounted and began kicking down doors.

A soldier called from a house. "There's no one here: the cowards must have slipped away in the night."

Erel furrowed her brow. "It doesn't make any sense. Why would the rebels stage here just to abandon it so quickly? Is their resolve truly so weak?"

Haynes shrugged and shook his head. His guess was as good as hers. "Stay with the men as they search the rest of town. I will ride to the reserve flank and inform command."

He left with a contingent of five men thundering back up the steep ridge to where the remaining forces were camped.

As they neared the top of the ridge, he heard metal clangs and groaning men, an unexpected commotion that made his heart drop. Those familiar sounds — shrieks of pain, cries of mercy, followed by a slash of the blade — triggered unwanted visuals in his mind. Haynes bit his lip and slowed his horse. Were those his men? And if so, how many had he lost?

Gaining up the ridge, he found the reserve force being slaughtered in a rear ambush led by a huge fighter clad in light chainmail and peasants wielding bows, pitchforks, and halberds as though it was death's own scythe. He watched the last few men go down. The field was strewn with bloody bodies, and his force was lost.

The men at his side, now rallied and boiling with anger, were ready to charge into this fleet of peasants who had slain their comrades. But Haynes held his arm out and began to wheel his horse around.

"Turn back," he ordered.

"But, sir—" The soldier was silenced by an arrow that lodged through his lower neck. The man next to him took one to the arm, and his mount suffered two blows. In a panic, the horse bucked and threw its rider off. The other mount, now riderless, bolted.

"Go, now!" Haynes repeated as he kicked his horse into a sprint. Arrows hissed past him, barely missing his arm and his mount by a hair. Holding the reins in a white-knuckle grip, he charged wildly back toward Rhea.

His steed slipped and stumbled but managed to stay upright as cries of horses and men behind him amplified. It was a bad idea to charge so fast over the damp ground, but what choice did he have? Haynes rounded the bend into town, and one horse following him fell victim to the slippery earth, falling over its rider.

The steed slid into Haynes' path and tripped his horse. He was thrown several feet, skidding out and tumbling into the mud. Haynes leapt to his feet, his sword drawn in a smooth motion in spite of the mud. His horse was kicking a broken leg as Haynes searched for his last standing man.

A riderless horse galloped out of the mist, passing him with arrows protruding from its neck. He could hear the enemy rushing down the slope on foot, the sound of a hundred raging men or more.

All the bravery he once had was gone with his horse. He turned and ran into the town, bellowing, "AMBUSH! REAR FORCES ARE LOST. PREPARE A SPEAR WALL!"

Erel perked her ears as she heard the familiar voice yelling from the edge of town. She turned her steed around and focused in the direction of Haynes' voice, but in the thick mist, she could barely make out anything.

"What was that?" Erel yelled back.

"AMBUSH. SPEARS. UP!"

Erel looked back at the cavalry lancers to her right. "You heard him. Go!"

They galloped forward, dozens of them in a synchronized line toward Haynes. They held one arm up with a shield over their heads, spears pointed up in the other. When they finally reached the sprinting commander, six cavalries split from the line and circled him, assembling a floral formation over Haynes' head.

Just a few seconds later, he heard a rain of arrows hit their shields like winter hail. The rest of the lancers had formed a border between Haynes and the incoming rebels. With spears out and shields blocking their way, the rebels, now visible in the hundreds over the ridge, came to a halt.

Erel and her steed charged into the ranks and reeled to a stop next to Haynes. She had a wild look to her. Haynes knew she was spoiling for a good fight. A surge of men poured in from behind, waiting for her command.

Haynes knew the gods wouldn't disappoint her on this day. He nodded to her, then called out for all to hear.

"Fighters, hear me," Haynes roared as he took Erel's side. "You are the strength of Althaea; you are the heart and soul of our people." He pointed his sword toward the sound of charging men. "Before you are those who would take this from you. They have come for your lives, wives, and children. Fight for the future of Althaea. This rebellion stops here and NOW!"

As he spoke, a huge arrow thudded into the chest of the lancer next to him, and he watched in horror as the man fell from his horse into the mud.

He looked around in search of the culprit on the ridge. Haynes' eyes were drawn to a gallant figure in the mist who stood out from the peasants that carried nothing but chainmail and gardening instruments. The warrior was clad in sturdy pauldrons and greaves, rims of gold along his vambrace, and a great Tatar bow in his hands.

Haynes cursed. "My Lord?"

Erel drew the same dark look on her face. "What's... going on?"

Rebel men came beside their new leader. Over the blue flag of Althaea, a banner raised with a bloody crest painted over the dark dragon. They had never seen this symbol before.

"He's joking, right?" Haynes stuttered as he glanced back and forth between Erel and Gaven. Erel's confusion had evolved into fear, then hate. But she was tasked to execute this plan, and she was going to see that the job was done one way or another.

"Draw your weapons," Erel commanded.

Haynes stammered, "W-w-what? Do you not see him?" He turned to Gaven, who raised his spear and pushed his white steed forward. Hundreds of men began to follow him out of the mist, walking, jogging, then running at the spear wall.

The first line of rebels to reach them were the bravest and most foolish. They threw themselves at the spear wall with abandon. For a moment, Haynes had confidence in their defenses, but when the earth erupted beneath the frontline and sent men and horses scattering aside, he was brought back to the reality that they were facing not only an enemy with overwhelming numbers but their own proud leader.

HAYNES HAD little time to wonder and even less to prepare. As the earth's crust rocked the ground, Erel was thrown from her mount, and Haynes fell on his bottom. A crazed fighter charged Haynes with an ax raised. He lifted the shield equipped on his left arm as the man hacked at him over and over, preventing Haynes from scrambling back to his feet.

Erel slipped in and out of the fray with a dagger and stabbed the man in the throat. She tossed Haynes her sword, nodded, and turned back to the fight. Her feet, lighter than dancing leaves, weaved through the opposing force. She pricked a needle-work pattern of violent red upon the enemy forces.

Haynes parried a short spear, pierced the heart of the wielder, kicked the man off of his sword, and cut a bloody swath through the next five men. The ferocity of the rebel attack shocked him. Many of them appeared to have little to no fighting experience, but what they lacked in technique, they made up for in brute strength and a thirst for blood.

Haynes heard his men cry out — blanketed in fear, disbelief, and hysteria — but he didn't know what to say.

A horrific shriek came from the white destrier as Gaven charged into the fight. It was then that Haynes knew where their spirit came from. Gaven cut through men and horses in single strokes. His strength and violence were so unbridled that he even caught overzealous rebels who fought too closely or were caught in his path. The entire rebel force went berserk.

Haynes leaped onto a riderless horse and charged at the Valiant Tiger. He gritted his teeth so hard that he tasted blood in his cheek. He steeled his heart for what he had to do – kill his leader before he killed all of their people.

Charging at the tiger's left flank, he scooped up a javelin from a rebel's hand and threw it at Gaven's back as hard as he could.

Gaven twisted in his saddle, batting the javelin aside with his forearm as he brought his spear around with his other hand. Haynes hardly raised his shield in time, and the blow sent him cartwheeling from his saddle into a group of rebel men.

Erel watched in horror as she saw the commander boldly go face-to-face with their leader. She turned back to the remaining men and ordered, "Ten men on me, the rest of you form a perimeter around Haynes!"

She didn't wait for the men to respond. Sprinting, she leaped onto the back of a wandering mount. She spurred the beast into a handful of rebels before she reached down and wrenched a sword from a dead body, taking a rebel's hand and half his face on the upswing. She slammed her horse into the crowd, slashing and hacking spears and swords, descending upon the commander.

Her horse knocked men aside as she swept the sword in elegant arcs, cutting a head from a spear followed by the wield-er's own. Six of her men were at her heels and kept the rebels at bay. She strutted her horse in front of Haynes while he recovered from the fall.

"You're insane!" She shamed the Valliant Tiger before charging, sword out and blade up as her weapon met his. The steels clashed, and the impact pulled their weapons upward. She readied the horse in his direction again and screamed, "Do you have anything to say for yourself?"

Gaven didn't respond to her taunts. He simply stared at her as if she was another enemy to be slaughtered.

"Answer me! Or answer to your men!" She gestured to the soldiers they had raised together, now losing limbs in an unexplained slaughter. They were distraught, shrinking in fear, some cowering behind their thin sticks of weapons.

"I fight… for the will of the gods," Gaven finally said. "It is fate that you all will be silenced here by my blade."

His declaration made Erel furrow her brow. Fate? Gods? She had never heard the atheist use such words.

Something else about him bothered her. The energy around them felt unusually grim, even malicious… more than any other battle she had fought before. Erel narrowed her eyes at her leader. It was different, but there was no doubt – that powerful aura came from him.

She focused on his heartbeat, pumping wildly; breathing, controlled and steady. She matched him, following a new rhythm until she met his pace…

But nothing happened. She stared bewildered at this stranger, one that she was now certain was not the Valiant Tiger she knew. In all her life, she'd never come across a person she couldn't shapeshift into, but whoever had taken over her leader had just added another tally. Two times in the span of a week. Something was going on, and she couldn't make sense of it.

The longer she stared at this new warrior, the more she saw how hollow his eyes were, gray and aimless, as if he couldn't see her. He seemed to be barely putting up an effort, letting Erel spend her energy fighting a pointless duel she was sure to lose.

But she wasn't going to play his game.

She roared, charging up to him again with her feet buckled tightly on the stirrup. Once their blades met, she abandoned her sword, reaching for his arm. With the help of her steed pushing forward, Erel yanked Gaven off his horse and let go. He landed flat on his back with damp mud all over his face.

Erel didn't stop. She went straight for Haynes, grasped him under his armpits and up onto her saddle.

"Cover us," she ordered the surrounding cavalry. "Archers, ready for retreat."

Her troops parted for her. The lancers charged forward in a sweep, knocking down anyone that met the end of their spear or the hoofs of their steeds. They circled back and followed Erel out. The archers stayed behind, readied their bows, and waited until all the cavalries were out of the way.

Before they could fire, a wall of mud and clay shot up around them. Frightened archers struck at the earth, and the harmless arrows were swallowed along with them.

Grains of sand fell onto Erel's back as they retreated, heading back to the capital. Tears bit her eyes as she heard her men take their last breath. She shed tears of sorrow for the lost men, tears of fear for the fate of the army, but most of all, she shed tears of rage for Gaven's betrayal.

CHAPTER SEVEN

News of the ambush at Rhea swept over the land like a prairie fire. Within a day, rumors of the Althaean region leader leading the commoner's rebellion spread across the alliance. What were once peaceful protests had now turned into a bloody battle as the rebellion grew from a movement to a revolution. With Gaven on their side, supporters across Althaea rallied faster than a plague.

Word of this madness quickly reached Solarin. No one was as shocked as Mirari when Joachim returned with the news. While she was busy looking for Salathiel, the real talk of the town was the riots in Althaea. Many feared the revolt would spread to the angsty peasants in Minetta, those who were just as displeased with the system.

But they were the minorities. Life in Minetta overall was better than in Althaea, their impoverished neighbor. Anyone who had an arm and a leg found work. Farmers sustained themselves and shared their resources. Those in the cities barely got by, but still, starvation was rare, and few had a reason to complain.

"The Council has declared the Valiant Tiger an outlaw," Joachim said as he tied his horse to a tree outside Mirari's cottage. "They say he's leading the rebellion. It's only going to get worse from here. For all we know, he really may be planning to take over the whole alliance. If it's true, it's only a matter of time before they catch him. I just want you to be mentally prepared."

Mirari was hoping that Joachim was just jesting to take her mind off Salathiel, except he never joked. She couldn't picture Gaven as a warmongering dictator.

"Gaven... would not do that," Mirari tried to reason with him. "He's born Minettan; he wouldn't attack us. This whole rebellion stuff... that's not like him."

"With all due respect, Milady, you haven't seen the child in over a decade. What he learned in Althaea, what he was trained to do, he may not be the person you remember him to be."

"Then perhaps I can talk some sense into him, make him stop before it gets out of hand."

"Lady Mirari," he cautioned. "That is not advisable."

"Maybe it's not what he really wants. Someone could be forcing him to do it." She paused, eyes widened. "Like... the Blessed?"

Though a month had passed since Salathiel's disappearance, she'd never stopped looking for him. The thought that she could possibly lose Gaven too stirred her nerves.

"The chances of that are very slim. The Blessed are silent killers, and this is a full-fledged war. But if His Honor has sided with the Blessed, it is even more reason not to get involved."

"Let me try. Please, Joachim. You told me to pick my battles. This is the battle I choose. I'm not going to stand by while the people who took care of me brawl with death."

"This is not your fight. We're talking about a battle against Althaea's greatest fighter and hundreds of his rebels, perhaps a thousand throughout the land. Something on this scale is no longer a personal matter. You have to leave it to the royal guards."

Mirari took a deep breath and uttered words she had not spoken in years. "That is an order, Joachim. Take me to Althaea."

Her resolve was direct, full of the confidence that she never had as a child. But now, as a woman, her eyes were filled with such determination that she was hardly the same little girl he once cared for. The certainty of her command, the force of her will – no one was going to hold down a maiden like that.

Words alone wouldn't have been able to change her mind. Salathiel and Gaven meant the world to her. After all, they gave her the companionship and acceptance her parents failed to provide, and she chose them over Joachim and the Hale family. He sighed.

"Stay there, Milady."

Joachim retreated to Salathiel's room, where he had laid his belongings for the duration of his stay. Bags and boxes were stacked to the roof, almost as if he had intended to live with her forever. But Mirari knew it was mostly clothes and weapons. He came back with a long wooden box. It was plain and unmarked, and for a second, she thought it was a big bottle of wine. He placed it on the table in front of Mirari and gestured for her to open it.

With the delicacy of handling a newborn, Mirari slid open the lid. There was a sword wrapped in black leather with cyan blue gemstones on the hilt. Mirari picked up the blade and unsheathed the weapon. It was lighter than the pots in her kitchen and much lighter than the sword Joachim trained her with years ago. There was a slight curve to it, and she stared at her reflection across its long edge.

"This was your father's," Joachim said. "He had this sword made when I was training him. Once you were old enough, it would become yours."

Mirari couldn't take her eyes off the beautiful blade. She carefully swung it around a few times, admiring its handling.

"My father knew how to wield a sword?"

"He wasn't good at it," Joachim admitted. "He always hoped you would have more use for that sword than he did."

A small chuckle escaped her. "Liar. My parents didn't want me to fight."

Joachim shrugged. "He knew that in this world, despite our advances in innovation and talks of peace, men will always be driven by bloodlust. The sword holds the most power in the alliance. If you can wield one, then you can change the future."

Mirari strode forward, blade coming down, rehearsing as if she was a warrior on the battlefield. When she turned her wrist, the blade flowed with her like it was cutting through wind. It fit her perfectly.

"Joachim, was that why you taught me how to fight? My father asked you to?"

"From the moment you were born, Lady Mirari... I knew you weren't the type of lady who sips buzzbean all day. Nothing ever stopped you from your ambitions."

Mirari stared at the blade, and for the first time, she noticed her parent's features within her own reflection – her sharp chin, much like her father, and her long, lilac hair that curled like ocean waves, just like her mother. Their reflection blurred as her eyes began to fill with tears. Mirari turned and wiped them away before Joachim would notice.

She cleared her throat and sheathed the sword. "So, we're going to Althaea?"

"If I say no, you will try to go on your own anyway." Now, she saw he was buckling on his own sword. "If we ride now, we may be able to make it to the border by dusk tomorrow. I hope you remember how to ride, Milady."

A STONE WALL higher than the tallest buildings of Fauna stretched from the Bay of Minetta to Lake Urabe, and it had stood there for nearly a millennium, dividing the land between Althaea and Minetta. From a distance in the desert, it looked like any other wall built by ancient ancestors. But as Joachim and Mirari got close enough to spot the kestrels of scouts circling the sky, they saw a shimmering coat of hāstals – with the transparent skin of glass jellyfish and the sting of its deadly tentacles – protecting the landmark.

The wall was as long as the trip they had made from Solarin, but there were only three gates – one on each end of the wall, and one at the center. The center gate was the one merchants and nobles took to cross into Ophallen, but it was emptier than usual.

A faint memory invaded Mirari's mind. Though she remembered little of it, Mirari once passed through this gate with Joachim and her parents. She only recalled hating a rude citizen whose toothless mouth reeked of an odor far worse than the littered streets. The rest weren't much different. She had begged to go home.

A score of female guards surrounded the single gate that allowed passage from Minetta to Althaea. It was unusual to see an all-women force, but that was the custom of the army of Oban, and they were as skilled and steadfast as any man, maybe more. They were covered with steel plates from head to toe and red capes bearing the flag of Minetta. The same design hung along the walls – a nimble fox, clever and protective like the people it represented.

The horse approached the gate but was quickly stopped by the surrounding guards. Lieutenant Quin told them, "The gate is closed until further notice."

"What do you mean it's closed?" Mirari demanded, putting on the fake noble attitude that came from being escorted on a horse.

"The Council has prohibited anyone from traveling to and from Althaea until the current situation is contained. Nobles included."

"Current situation? You mean about Ga... Region Leader Gaven?"

"We cannot allow Minettans to get involved, Miss. Please turn around."

Mirari glanced back at the border gate, examining the walls. She thought maybe she could use her wind kore to push herself over the top, but the chances of her being able to reach that high were slim to none – either the energy protecting the wall or the fall would surely kill her.

Mirari looked at the guards equipped with javelins and saber-lions, all ready to hit her if she dared try to fight them. She was determined to get through that gate by any means necessary. She felt a false sense of confidence with her hand resting on the hilt of her sword.

Joachim pivoted the horse away from the gate and whispered to Mirari. "It won't do any good to argue with them."

"You have a better idea?"

Joachim looked around and was drawn to an elegant black carriage coming up from behind them. It looked odd. Its unique gold and pink design was in contrast to most carriages that were either white or brown. The carriage was intercepted by another group of guards, forcing it to come to a halt. A handful of papers poked out the window, and the guards took it. It drew the atten-tion of Lieutenant Quin, and with a tight grip around her spear, she approached the carriage.

Squinting through the fug of dust, Joachim began to trot the horse toward the carriage. "I think I know them."

"Of course you know them. Is there a single noble family in Minetta you don't know?"

Lieutenant Quin examined the crinkled papers, spending an

excessive amount of time on one page with a golden seal. She nodded and waved the guards to stand aside.

Mirari furrowed her brow, got off the horse, and stomped toward the carriage. "By the blood-soaked tunics of clam diggers, I thought you said this border was closed."

"It is," said Lieutenant Quin.

"Really? So why do they get to pass?" But the lieutenant ignored her, handing the papers back to the person inside the carriage.

Mirari peeked inside and saw a delicate woman with a curtain of rose-kissed hair and charms around her wrists that suggested she was a healer. She was accompanying… what Mirari thought was a man, covered in chainmail and face hidden behind a silver mask. His clothes suggested that he was a warrior, but he had a thin figure resembling a woman's and garments oddly casual enough to suggest that the person could also be a servant.

The odd man waved upon seeing Joachim on the other side of the carriage, and they engaged in a quiet discussion that Mirari could not hear. She then turned her attention to the young noble sitting across from him.

He was in frilled attire, handsomely fit with a few blains along the side of his face. By the look of it, he was the master of the house. If his goal was to not be seen, he was doing an excellent job. He meditated on the shadows underneath his leather shoes, showing off the brown curls over his heavy brow ridge. He was taking far more interest in the carriage's panels than the people around him.

But he looked up, eyes locked on Mirari for longer than she was comfortable with. Mirari was about to scowl at him until he said, "Let her pass."

Lieutenant Quin looked back at Mirari, almost unwilling to acknowledge her mistake.

"Sir, she needs proper documentation to pass."

The masked man turned to the guard and waved her aside, saying, "She will be under my supervision. The Council will understand."

"Yes, sir," the lieutenant said with a bow.

Mirari marveled at how easy it was for him but still questioned who was the true leader of this trio.

"Invite your lady in, Joachim," the man said. Joachim didn't waste a second in dismounting from his horse – practically giving it to the guards for free – and opened the door for Mirari.

"Sorren, come over here." The lady patted the tiny space next to her, and the boy made way for their new guests.

Inside the carriage, Mirari could see the man more clearly – dull silver armor and worn-out red cloak, shabby for a man with such power. His head was tilted in her direction. She assumed he was looking at her, but he said nothing. What made him important was surely as mysterious as why he wore a mask. Seeing how odd the man looked, Mirari understood why they got special attention.

The guards stepped aside as the carriage bustled in, entering into Althaean territory. They were a single carriage in a sea of dried earth. The lack of shrubbery and empty terrain projected an eerie feeling — the most lonesome place and the least desirable spot to have a cart malfunction — but Mirari knew this was the calm before the storm. Whether or not she believed she could succeed in reaching Gaven, there was no turning back now.

CHAPTER EIGHT

Mirari decided to rest for the evening, speaking little to the strangers who had helped them. All she knew was that the healer and masked man were married and were from the northern region of Avon. Their names were Fangbane and Starlight, and the younger one was Sorren.

It was obvious they were fake names, but as someone who also hid her real identity, she didn't have the right to judge them. The Council had invited them to fight the rebellion, so they must be important one way or another.

Mirari introduced herself as Joachim's friend, and a dear friend to Region Leader Gaven. She explained that she wanted to talk Gaven out of whatever he was doing. As preposterous as her mission sounded, the couple didn't ask any questions, only nodded and smiled. Their unconditional support felt suspicious.

The morning light disturbed her slumber. When she awoke, her head was on Joachim's shoulder – not much different from when she was a child. He was wide awake, looking out the window. He never slept, or at least he knew how to sleep with his eyes open.

The couple was also fast asleep, taking support of each

other's heads while Sorren slept against the carriage wall. The man seemed to never take off his mask. Mirari wondered if his wife was okay with that, but she seemed at peace, comfortably wrapped in her husband's arms. Despite their strange chemistry, it was clear they had complete trust in each other.

Mirari looked out the window. They were approaching a small town – it was a destitute scene, as expected. When she'd traveled to Althaea as a child, her parents always stayed clear of shabby places like the neighborhood they were passing through.

As they entered the town of Naiad, on the edge of the Ophallen region, the streets got worse – filthy, polluted, and every building an eyesore. She noticed many of the shops and homes had been broken or damaged. One bakery had a cracked window but was still bustling with business.

The smell was wretched; rats darted about the rotting garbage strewn on the streets. But the sorriest sight was of the ragged skeletons – starving homeless folk, hollow-eyed and unwashed, occupying every corner. Mirari did her best to ignore all the misery and focused on her quest. But the obvious plight of the citizens tore at her heart.

"Don't worry," the boy said, now barely awake with his head still pressed against the wall. "The future I see only gets better from here."

Mirari tilted her head. His demeanor wasn't any more normal than the other two next to him. Still, she had to ask him, "Why did you let me come with you, Young Lord?"

"If I didn't, you would've fought the guards. I had to put you on the right track. The next decision is Nanaka, by the way."

"Decision? What decision are you—"

"And I'm not a lord. You do not have to address me as such."

Mirari raised a brow. "But—"

"A lord has servants and we do not. It's just the three of us."

Mirari glanced at the couple fast asleep. "Are they your parents?"

"We are here to stop a rebellion. That's all there is to it."

Mirari smiled at the strange boy. She recognized that youthful disobedience, his desire to make something of himself without being tied down to the wishes of those around him. Even if she couldn't understand him, she sensed nothing but pure intentions.

The coach drew up at a sprawling military encampment outside Naiad. She could see tents, horses, wagons, and hundreds of troops, company after company, stretched into the distance. What impressed her the most was that they were soldiers from every empire, indicated by the multitude of banners and insignia from Althaea, Minetta, and even Valenia. For them all to be in one place, sharing the same grub and tents – she never thought such a sight was possible.

Fangbane, who had now awoken, saw her gazing in wonder and said, "It is the first time troops from all over have come together to cooperate on a single mission."

Mirari blinked. She was sure she hadn't said those thoughts out loud. She shook it off and asked, "But how... I mean, who brought them all together? The Council?"

"They approved, yes. I put up a rather good argument for my idea. After all, if this rebellion isn't stopped, it could spread across every empire."

"Your idea? You pulled all this together?" Mirari marveled, now seeing why he was so important. He was the leader of this whole operation, and she ran into him by luck. But she wondered if they needed these many people to stop Gaven.

"This is our meeting point, but some will go off to help fight the rebellions in other regions," Fangbane spoke up, interrupting Mirari's flow of thoughts once again. She furrowed her brow, unsure if the second time was a coincidence. She wanted to ask how he knew what she was thinking, but their carriage pulled to a halt, and their door swung open.

Joachim stepped out first, reaching a hand out to help Mirari down, then Starlight. They were greeted by a young lieutenant, whose bow-like insignia showed he was from the Tribe of Aegises in Valenia. He stepped up to salute Fangbane.

"Sir, they are meeting in the logistics room." He pointed at a tent large enough for a circus, with red, blue, and gray banners.

"Thank you, Lieutenant. See that the others get some refreshments."

"Yes, sir," he said, followed by another crisp salute.

"I pity you, Mirari," Sorren said almost in a whisper. "To have to take the life of someone so dear to you. The curse you live with is... more heartbreaking than my own."

Mirari kept still. The boy's words began to mold from strange to eerie. What was he referring to? But before she could ask, Starlight nudged him over toward a tent right behind Joachim and the lieutenant. Fangbane grabbed Mirari by the arm and escorted her in the opposite direction.

"Come along. We're late."

"We?"

"Of course. You're here to help stop the Valiant Tiger, are you not? I dare say you have an idea or two yourself, don't you?"

Of course, she did. That was all she thought about during the long ride to the border, but her plans involved only her, Joachim, and a heart-to-heart talk with an old friend. As ludicrous and fairytale-like as it sounded, she believed that was all she needed to do to make Gaven put an end to this rebellion.

She didn't expect to be pitching any of it to other fighters. And now, here was the other problem — she was a simple peasant, one that had never seen a battlefield, and she knew she would stand out like a domestic cat in a pack of wolves.

"I'd rather do this alone," Mirari said, pulling her arm from him.

"Perhaps I wasn't clear." His tone grew tense, and Mirari felt her body grow stiff. "You must remain by my side at all times. That is not negotiable."

Mirari crossed her arms. "Like a slave? I didn't come here to join the army."

"Then you'll at least pitch your plans to the fighters, hm? I reckon since you were planning to do this by yourself, you have an idea of where he is."

"I… maybe? But how——"

"Great. Then come along." He gestured again to the tent. "Who knows. Maybe they'll agree. More support for you, the better, right? Either way, you are not to see the Valiant Tiger on your own. Even if you convince him to stand down, there's no guarantee that the rebels won't try to take your life."

Mirari lowered her eyes, realizing her ignorance for failing to see that possibility. Now, seeing how many people were involved in this mission, she was convinced it wasn't wise to go in alone, even if Gaven used to be like a brother to her. But she had no military experience, no idea what to expect inside that tent, and she doubted if people would be willing to believe her that Gaven was innocent.

She followed Fangbane inside. Her ears erupted with the deep booms of muscular men and prideful women. Nearly three dozen decorated fighters and their guards were milling around in groups, each in animated discussion. They were no doubt masters of one out of the four fighter styles – paragon, umbra, celta, and aegis. If their physiques and garments weren't intimidating enough, their signature weapons, strapped to their belts, decorated in gold and fine glazes, made Mirari certain that if a fight broke out in this tent, she would surely die.

Fangbane gravitated to the first person he saw, a fairly young man with a roguish look, hair tied back in a high ponytail. Behind him was a larger fellow that could've been mistaken for a gritbear. He wore a pair of pewter gauntlets larger than Mirari's head and dark shades above his bright smile. Mirari recognized the swirled insignia on their shoulders – fighters from Avon.

Her attention wandered to a small group of officers next to

her. Their armor was different from the rest, trimmed in gold and polished with reflective oil. They wore a darker shade of metal, iconel alloys, Mirari assumed, an expensive and hard-to-obtain material reserved for the most valuable fighters. These fighters had blue cloaks, and that in itself made Mirari feel uncomfortable. For all she knew, they had already exchanged insults behind her back.

"Gaven isn't listening," said the man with a lock of wavy crimson hair. Mirari didn't intend to eavesdrop, but hearing his name in an informal manner caught her attention. When she glanced at the man, she noticed his small, dark eyes and half his face sunk into his tall collar. But his voice didn't project the same emotion. He yapped as if he was ready to execute the next person who disagreed with him.

That would be the fair lady, old enough to be his mother and decorated with wrinkles across her otherwise flawless, snowy skin. She didn't seem afraid of him one bit.

"I trained that child." The woman spat with such defiance that the intimidating man looked away. "True, he had always cared about the common people, but he would never turn against his own army. I want to speak to him myself before we start spreading any more preposterous rumors."

The corner of Mirari's lip perked up. She was thankful to know that there were people who agreed with her.

"Councilor Suzan, with all due respect, he has hacked his way across three villages in just two days, all of which have reported the same. It's no rumor. Your protégé has gone rabid."

Mirari couldn't stop herself from listening to them now. Since they had similar armor, she figured that the person next to Councilor Suzan must also be a councilor.

"Eavesdropping on councilors is a crime, you know that?" Mirari heard an unfamiliar voice. She noticed that there was now a finely-toned fighter before her. He had a long scarf with a pattern of teal fish scales over his navy suit, tailored with more cerulean gemstones than she could count. His black umbra gloves hovered over a selection of fine daggers, throwing stars, and the winged-crown insignia of Axillaire in gold stitching. He had a naughty grin on his face – mischievously handsome behind his copper hair – a smile that told Mirari that he was more than ready to offer her a bargain to dismiss her crime.

He leaned close to look over her head and noticed the feathered pin in her hair. Mirari was waiting for him to make some Minettan joke – her glare dared him to – but he dismissed it as if she was everything he expected.

"You don't seem to be a fighter," he began, eyes drifting down to her chest and ogling her thin garments. "Why are you here? Are you a spy? Someone's concubine?"

If he had been some impolite scum on the streets of Solarin, she would've sacked his treasures in a split second, but her position in a tent full of nobles and the most powerful fighters across the alliance made her powerless.

"I… came here with him." Mirari nodded her head toward the masked man, who had his back turned to them.

"Ah, the tin can. I didn't know he was bringing along ladies of the night. In that case, if you have any openings tonight—"

"We're about to get started, Ahden," a gentleman snapped before Mirari could defend herself. He and Suzan had now joined their discussion, only they seemed to ignore Mirari's presence. "Stop flirting with every woman in this tent and take your seat."

"Have a little fun, brother," the umbra jested. "It's not every day you get such a fine selection of foreign maidens all in one place."

Brother? Mirari thought they looked nothing alike, and their personalities were opposites. She couldn't even tell who was the younger one, but the councilor looked like an elder wolf trying to calm an energetic pup.

The councilor grabbed his brother by the collar and dragged

him to a long mahogany table, which the herd of fighters surrounded. The seats were unmarked, plain as they should be for an emergency setup, but the fighters each grabbed a chair as if they had rehearsed it. They knew exactly where to sit, who to sit next to, and they cascaded into an order sorted by the vibrant capes on their back.

The one person who didn't take a seat was, to no surprise, the masked man. Mirari had been nursing a hint of skepticism, believing that it was too good to be true that he was the leader of the pack, but now she saw it. The greatest leaders across the alliance, even members of the Council, gave their undivided attention to this man.

But Fangbane looked at Mirari, not intimidatingly but invitingly. He pulled up the chair at the end of the table and patted the top rail. All eyes turned to her now, waiting for her to take her seat. Flustered red with embarrassment, she hustled to the chair with her eyes glued to the ground and sat down.

Fangbane spoke, spouting details and terminology that went over Mirari's head. He kept pointing to an enormous map, sweeping his pointer from here to there, going on and on about tactics. Something about circling towns, covering land and sea. Fangbane wasn't just commanding the team designated to capture Gaven; he was also dictating how other teams should help contain the growing riots across Althaea.

Many argued that the army should be sent to protect the largest cities instead of trying to chase the rebels all over the countryside in a hundred directions. Others insisted that the only way to stop the rebels was to wage a scorched earth campaign – destroy their homes, their crops, their families, everything. Without supporters to feed them, with no homes or families to fight for, they couldn't hold out for long. They would lose heart and accept defeat.

Fangbane didn't agree with any of their ideas.

He faced a lot of friction as far as commanding his assembly of troops. There were arguments between regional armies, squabbles among leaders, old scores to settle, and of course, no shortage of ambitious officers who saw their chance to make their career, even at the expense of their fellow officers.

Mirari began to wonder if she would have to wait until sundown before they got to talking about Gaven. She was pulled out of boredom by a graceful woman who sat next to her.

"You're from Minetta, aren't you?" she whispered as her lilac hair fell to the side of her face like a blanket of silk.

"Yes, madam." Mirari now raised her head, getting a good look at the lady. To her surprise, the lady looked younger than her, with scrawny arms and baby cheeks that puffed up with her smile. She wore a silver crown over her forehead, one of those that doubled as a protective helmet. On her shoulder was a familiar snake-like insignia. This lady looked nothing like the menacing guards she met at the Althaean-Minettan border. The smile over her freckles told Mirari that she wouldn't kill a bug.

"Don't worry about formalities. I'm Iphigenia. I serve Region Leader Nivenda of Minetta. You can call me Iffy."

"I'm Mirari. I'm just a merchant from Avon."

"Mirari. Wow, I love it." Iphigenia's face glowed up. "The Goddess of Miracles. That was my great-grandmother's name. I haven't met anyone else with that name till now." Her gaze shifted to a man across the table. "I couldn't help but overhear your conversation earlier with Region Leader Ahden. If Fang-bane brought you here, you must be very important."

Mirari swallowed, not realizing Ahden was a region leader. She glanced at him, growing flustered from their earlier conversation. As for why Mirari was in this meeting…

"I'm… not quite sure I'm that important," she said.

They were interrupted by men yelling across the table. Ahden rose from his seat and directed his attention to a muscular giant, blond with a bulging chin, four seats away at the far end of the table. He damned the brawler for raising his voice, and the brawler too rose from his seat, ready to take on the challenge.

"No, no, a valid question," Fangbane said in a calm voice. "Your skepticism is justified, Commander Reiss, and I'd be more than happy to leave you in charge of the front to silence the growing crowd in Xeran."

The bearded giant sunk back in his chair, speechless by how agreeable Fangbane was. But Ahden stayed up, hands on his hip as if he were showing off the gems on his leather belt.

"Really, Tin Can?" said Ahden. "Why would you let a swine handle my territory?"

"Because we need your godly presence rallying the maidens at the main battle, My Good Lord," Fangbane said. "The Tribe of Paragons can practically see Axillaire from their own front yard. Surely they are familiar with the terrain. You can rest assured your region is safe in their hands."

Ahden was silenced, too embarrassed to admit that Fangbane had the right idea. He played it off, keeping his chin high as he sank back into his seat, reminding his peers that he was far more important than the brute he just yelled at.

Iphigenia whispered in Mirari's ear, "He tends to say a little more than he should. Don't mind him. Everyone here thinks they're the smartest person in the tent. If you ever feel uncomfortable around Ahden, just make your complaint to Councilor Adder. Minettan or not, he'll believe you."

Mirari pondered, now knowing the name of the reserved man that sat next to Ahden. "Why is he in a gloom?"

"Councilor Adder? Oh no, that's just how he looks, sweetie. Don't let that deceive you. He can command a crowd."

The attention at the table swept to the cerulean celta sitting next to Adder, who challenged Fangbane's unusual method of capturing the Valiant Tiger. He was a severe-looking man with his arms crossed against his chest. Behind his round, golden glasses, Mirari could tell that not only was he intelligent, but he had a lot of pride. His light blue hair, a feature common among healers and spellcasters, meant that he was...

"Kieran from the Tribe of Celtas," Iphigenia said as they watched him bicker with Fangbane. "He's one of the best healers of the tribe."

"Do you really think all these people from different empires can work together?" Mirari whispered back. "It hardly seems like they can agree on anything."

"That's just the nature of the war room. Yes, it is quite a stretch, but Fangbane has a good handle on things, don't you think?"

Mirari nodded. He was able to put every fighter at ease as if he knew what they wanted to hear and what would satisfy them enough to silence them.

Kieran adjusted his glasses, shaking his head. He was a little harder to persuade than the rest. "This fool takes us for pathetic incompetents. Althaea said they didn't want any help."

"I second this," a lady in a blue cloak from the far end of the table spoke up. "We didn't ask for the swine's help."

"With all due respect, you do need help." All eyes turned to the roguish umbra Mirari saw earlier. He sat two seats down from Iphigenia, at the center of Minetta's side of the table. His glare was enough to silence the Althaean. He countered her without a shred of respect. "You failed to control the situation, and now the other empires are at risk of a revolt. Suck up your pride and admit you blew it."

Kieran, on the other hand, was not fazed. He said, "You're not in any position to say that, Shadow Soldier."

Mirari marveled at the Shadow Soldier — Shiba Zabato, the Region Leader of Avon. The glare from his crimson eyes was as haunting as they said.

"Cut it out, you two," Adder warned, with the delicacy of his soothing voice, barely loud enough for everyone to hear. But his words were enough to silence anyone in the room. This method had always worked for him, except against one person.

"Good brother, I normally have no issues with the decisions you and Suzan make," Ahden wheedled to Adder. "But putting your trust in a drunk and a man who won't show his face is beyond ridiculous."

"I dare you to say that again, flatty," Shiba said.

"Alright, that's enough." Suzan clapped her hands, gesturing to Fangbane. "Adder and I put our full trust in this man. If you don't like it, you're more than welcome to leave and join the others marching to Xeran."

No one dared to argue this, not only because they didn't wish to defy the Council, but they also didn't want to be left out of the exclusive team of fighters. They had a chance to shine, and they were ready to show off.

CHAPTER NINE

Hours had passed, and now only a dozen or so leaders were left in the room. The others had been dispatched to lead rescue teams to counter the growing riots across Althaea.

Fangbane could tell that Mirari was ready to take an afternoon nap. He watched as her mind drifted, thinking of all the possible things she would say to Gaven once she met him. She wanted to tell him about her clients in Solarin and how much better she was at holding a sword. Should she go for a handshake or a hug? How would she go about telling him about Salathiel's disappearance? Or her new name? Then she melted into a sulk, thinking of what Salathiel would say about her dangerous endeavor and the last moments he was with her. She vowed to find Salathiel, but right now, Gaven needed her help. A single tear escaped her eye before anyone else could notice.

"Have we figured out why the Valiant Tiger is acting this way?" Iphigenia asked. "This isn't like him at all."

Everyone's attention was now drawn to a petite lady with a brownish bob sitting next to Fangbane, as stiff and composed as a doll. The dragon crest of Althaea Main over her dark tunic made her role clear.

"This is his second in command, Lady Erel." Fangbane introduced her to the fighters left at the table. She kept her head low, then took a deep breath, exuding command as she relayed her story.

"An assassin infiltrated our inner walls a few days ago," she said, directing her attention to the fighters. "He had a strange power, one that could numb your body, send your mind into a hallucination, and put malicious voices in your head. He attacked both His Honor and me. I recovered, but ever since His Honor woke up, he hasn't acted the same."

"So what? We're going to blame it on insanity? Mind-control?" Ahden taunted.

"It's not a myth," Kieran spoke up. "You may not have heard of such experiences, but it would not be the first time we've come across something capable of polluting one's mind. There are many toxins in this world we have yet to study."

"You are missing the point!" Ahden shouted. "I, for one, don't give a bucket of Nanakan fish guts why Gaven turned into a mad dog. All that matters is that we bring this mongrel to heel."

A celta on Ahden's side of the table, elegantly clad with at least a dozen necklaces and pendants hanging from her neck, each bearing an icon of Oris, spoke up. She had stayed out of the debate this entire time, but something had captured her interest. She stood up, brushed her pigtail braids behind her back, and curtsied.

"Commander Ridge of Evaleen, Lady Erel," she said, barely able to keep her head up. "I-If I may, can you describe more of this man's power?"

Erel nodded. "As far as I could tell, it wasn't a spell or kore for that matter. Wherever it came from, he was able to conjure a dark mist from his hands."

"And did it give you an… out-of-body experience?"

Erel blinked a few times. "Yes. Yes, it did."

"Ah…" Ridge looked like she was ready to confirm her diagnosis but held back.

"Well?" Kieran prodded. "Out with it."

"In Plethorist mythology, such symptoms were known to be caused by dark aura." Hearing this, the room fell silent. Most were confused, but a few had gone pale. The fact that Ridge had acknowledged a religion outside her own was a sin. "It may be the work of—"

"Don't say it." Kieran held up his hand. "You know better." Ridge nodded and sat back down with her head lowered. But not everyone knew what they were speaking of.

"What are you so shy about, lizard face?" Commander Reiss said. "Is it the work of another one of your poisonous witches? That aster spellcaster? I told you she was still alive."

Kieran's face began to redden, his eyes scowling at the enemy of his clan.

"Don't pin everything on that poor woman!" Iphigenia interrupted. "The Witch of Aten doesn't tinker with psychosis. She's an alchemist. You already knew this, Reiss. Besides, your people sent assassins after her into our territory, did you not? Another word of this, and I will press charges."

Commander Reiss was silent. But a man like him wasn't going to give up. His gaze drifted to the ladies next to Iphigenia. "What about the little runt? What does she contribute?"

"Hey!" Erel hissed, standing up and pulling a dagger from her belt. She twirled the weapon, daring him to insult her again.

"Not you. I'm talking about that peasant in front of you."

Everyone at the table looked at Mirari. She sat frozen like a deer.

"I… I can fight," Mirari said, but it wasn't the brightest thing to say in a room full of the best. There was a snicker from at least one person in the tent.

"She's with me," Fangbane said, diverting the attention in the room back to him. "She helped me come up with our current strategy…"

I did? She hadn't said a word about her plan.

"And she'll be helping me execute it henceforth."

I'll… what?

This sent whispers around the table. "Mirari, would you like to explain your plan now?"

"Me?" she hissed. *I haven't even told you—*

"No, no. Go on. I trust you."

"Um…" Mirari slowly rose from her seat and walked to the front of the map. Now would not be the time to trip or stutter. Her hands trembled as she took a deep breath and said, "We need to know the Valiant Tiger's next location."

"Thanks for pointing that out," a voice shouted from the back. He was hushed by the person next to him.

Iphigenia whispered, "Introduction first, darling."

She froze as if someone had pierced an arrow through her neck. Mirari cleared her throat and started again, now speaking a little louder. "My name's Mirari Zanette of Avon, and I have an idea of where the Valiant Tiger may be." But Fangbane knew she didn't have a plan; she had a series of hypotheses. Which would be the right one? He wanted her to stimulate his brain. Mirari scanned the terrain on the map, using the little of what she knew from reading books on Althaean war history. She pointed to the center of the map. "We are here in Naiad. This encampment protects everything to the West, and with the Army of Ophallen protecting the borders, Gaven's forces wouldn't be going toward Minetta. He was last seen in the villages around Rhea, so he would be heading north to Evaleen or south to Axillaire."

"Definitely Axillaire," one fighter called out.

"Shut it, Larson." Ahden snapped. "It's clearly Evaleen."

Mirari's attention was on the hills on the other side of the Yountilla River. Anyone would be daft to march toward the ocean, but they couldn't ignore the land across the Gulf of Oris. Fangbane watched Mirari measure the distance of the gulf with her finger to confirm her theory. Her eyes widened.

"He's going to Nanaka," Mirari said. When she uttered those words out loud, she realized. *Sorren was right.*

"Entering Valenia through the Gulf of Oris," Fangbane nodded, impressed. "If he knows our forces are stationed along the border of Ophallen, he can either move inland to the Valenian border or north to Altha Hills. But the farther north he moves, the more he'll run out of land, and trying to cross the warded Althaean-Valenian border wall will be suicide. Nanaka makes sense."

"That would be laughable," Kieran said, flicking his hand in the air. "As if the Tribe of Celtas would let that happen."

"With all due respect, Sir Kieran, in the face of mana neutralizers, your tribe will be able to do little."

"What was that? Mana neutralizers? As if some peasant rebels would have weapons like that."

"But…" Mirari pondered. "What if he picked up some along the way?"

Fangbane rubbed his chin, realizing the area surrounding the gulf was full of imports. He said, "They'll stop by an armory first."

Weapons were Gaven's favorite thing. If anyone understood the value of good armor and a sharp blade, it was him. There was no way the rebels could stand up to any regional army unless they had the real armaments. But equipped with thousands of the best swords, shields, arrows, and armor, it was anyone's game.

"I don't follow," Kieran said.

"Your Graces," Fangbane turned to Councilor Suzan and Adder. "Are there any armories in the area between Rhea and the Gulf of Oris?"

"In Allore?" Adder pondered, turning his gaze to Suzan.

"No, too small," Suzan said. "There's not enough special

weaponry there to be useful to an army as large as Gaven's forces. He wouldn't waste his time going for something so insignificant."

"Wasn't a shipment of hāstal weaponry being set up at Ganmali?"

Ahden leaned back to the bulky spellcaster behind him and whispered in his ear. Someone handed Ahden several papers, which he scanned quickly until he found something that interested him.

"Five dozen crates of armor, swords, and arrows left our ports this morning," he said. "Including mana neutralizers. That means they'll be at the Ganmali Armory by tomorrow morning."

"I call dibs on the tiger's head," a paragon shouted from the back.

Another voice rang out, "Clearly, the better fighter deserves to claim the kill, and that would be me."

"Wait, we can't kill him," Mirari said, but her soft voice drowned in the tent of battle-hard fighters.

The hot-headed Shadow Soldier stood up. "If anyone's doing the killing, it'll be me, and you know it! You all owe Minetta this much."

But more opposition drowned the room, few respecting Shiba.

"You featherpits and swines stay out of this!" Ahden yelled. "Have you forgotten you are on Althaean land? This is our battle. We will be the ones to take him down."

"No one will be doing any killing!" Fangbane yelled.

"What do you mean, Tin Can?" Ahden said. "He's leading a bloody rebellion. You may not be familiar with this, but in Althaea, we don't give exceptions to those who betray the system, not even region leaders."

"He doesn't know what he's doing," Erel said in almost a hiss. "Give us a chance to talk to him and sort things out."

But there was another prize to be won. Erel wasn't a region

leader, hence she had little power in the room. But if the Valiant Tiger was slain in battle, then she would assume his role... and she looked like an easy kill for the throne.

"The time for chit-chat ended when he betrayed his duty!"

"Slay the tiger!"

"Althaea knows no mercy!"

"Silence!" Suzan's cane whipped the table, whose wooden surface began to crack. "He shall be taken in alive. No exceptions."

"Are you going to play favoritism here, Suzan?" Ahden said.

"It's not favoritism, brother," Adder said. "Upon hearing Miss Ridge's statement, we've decided to have the man put to trial. He is to be brought in alive."

"What, are you seriously believing the mind-control bull crap?" a Valenian brawler shouted.

"If you disagree, I am more than happy to relay your thoughts to Councilor Julie." The brawler shuddered.

Fangbane patted Mirari on the back and gestured to her to step aside. She was more than willing to.

"If the Valiant Tiger knew the shipment schedule, then that means he's already on his way. Rally your teams," Fangbane said as he grabbed his coat. "I'll explain the rest on the way."

CHAPTER TEN

F angbane decided to gamble – not on his own hunch but on
military reality. He believed Mirari's theory and was certain
a clever opponent like Gaven would surely see the Ganmali
Armory as the solution to his lack of weapons.

A company of five thousand men and their commanders
followed Fangbane's orders and broke camp, moving east at a
forced march. They had to reach Ganmali before the rebels in
order to ambush them before they got their hands on the massive
cache of weapons that would turn the tide in their favor.

But to move five thousand heavily-equipped men was no easy
campaign, especially compared to Gaven's rebels who only
carried chainmail and a pitchfork at most.

"We won't move fast enough," Suzan said as she brought her
horse next to Fangbane. They took the lead, while others stayed
with their commanding groups. To his side, Starlight was
conversing with Ridge, Kieran, and other medics designated for
the campaign. He left that division in her lead.

"Not fast enough… under these current circumstances,"
Fangbane said. "Which is why we must change the
circumstances."

"And how do you propose to do that? Grow wings?"

"The light brigade," Fangbane said.

"And what in Inferna is that?"

Fangbane smiled.

Taking a fraction of their army, Fangbane would send swift, small groups to harass and stall Gaven's forces.

"We stir up just enough chaos and confusion to slow them down," he said. "Hit them hard, then pull out."

"And all the while, you're buying time for us to maneuver the main force to Ganmali?" Suzan said. "You are as clever as they say, Fangbane. Or should I just call you Commander Fang?"

"Whatever you'd like, Your Grace," he chuckled. "But I'm no commander. I just see possibilities others may deem impossible."

Mirari had more she wanted to say to Fangbane, but he was busy with the councilors. She was a little ways behind on her mount, alongside Iphigenia and Joachim, waiting for an opportunity. Mirari turned to Iphigenia only to realize she, too, was gone, trailing a few paces behind with a dark-skinned giant. Iphigenia gestured over to Mirari, and now he was looking at her too.

This was the first time she saw him by his distinguishable features, and the fact that he stood next to his partner at all times indicated exactly who he was: the Silver Fist, second in command and partner of the Shadow Soldier. He was as fit and muscular as they said, twice the size of Shiba's skinny frame. His dark skin complemented his white hair, and the broad smile he flashed at Mirari was enough to convince her that he was a friendly person.

"Well, well. Welcome, young lady!" He and Iphigenia galloped to her. "Mirari, was it?"

"Yes, My Lord."

"No, no. Neo will do." Neo let out a merry chuckle and nodded toward the man next to him, the Shadow Soldier. "As for that miserable sourpuss, you can just call him Shiba. You have my permission."

"You do not," Shiba mumbled. She noticed he was nipping

at a silver flask of brandy. "I've never heard of a Mirari in our army. Are you sure you're from Avon, or are you just lying?"

"Shiba…" His partner warned, then turned back to the lady. "Mirari is kind of a mouthful. Mind if I just call you M?"

"If you like."

"Thanks, M." Then, he addressed Shiba. "She might be here for other reasons. No rule saying that this fight is only for region leaders and their commanders." Mirari was immediately fond of the playful giant. But she could see the disdain in his partner's eyes.

"As if we weren't being embarrassed enough," Shiba said. "He brings her along."

"We don't know what she has to offer yet," Neo said. Mirari wished she had an answer to that herself.

Shiba said, "If you're not a fighter, then why are you here? You can't lie in a room full of elites." Mirari's heart skipped a beat, wondering if he had figured out that she was a Hale. But instead of her face, he pointed to the black sword strapped around her waist. "A good sword doesn't make up for lack of skill. Your aura. It's weak. I bet you've never even seen blood. No one is going to hold your hair back when you puke on the battle-field. Just stick to the whorehouse."

"I…" Mirari stopped herself from lashing out because he was her region leader. "I know how to use it. I'll duel you to prove it."

The corner of his lip perked up, almost as if he was waiting for her to say it. The thrill of a duel aroused him. She instantly regretted it. His crimson eyes reminded her he was a shadow-mancer, a man with a deadly skill that would make her the target of two opponents. She had no experience with that. And if she lost, would he send her home? Kill her on the spot? She couldn't risk it.

But before Shiba could answer, his giant bellowed a loud

chuckle that would've been enough to wake the whole forest for miles.

"Okay, Shiba. That's enough brandy for today." He gently nudged the grumbling leader forward. Neo gave a friendly goodbye wave to Mirari as they trotted ahead.

"Don't mind Shiba," Iphigenia said once they were out of sight. "He's always a grump."

Mirari didn't think so. She only ever heard good things about him and the rest of the Zabato family that had ruled Avon for centuries. Very few peasants made complaints against the army, and she knew most of the people in Solarin had no problem with the Shadow Soldier.

"What changed him?" Mirari asked.

Iphigenia's cheery tone was gone, replaced with pity. "He lost more than he can handle. Please forgive him. He's still a good person. He just… hasn't quite found his way back yet."

Even though she didn't know the details, Mirari took those words to heart. She knew what it was like to deal with a loss. Salathiel's disappearance still left an open wound in her soul. Even now, when her focus was Gaven, she still grieved for Salathiel. And when she saw Shiba, a man who had completely lost himself in anger and grief, she couldn't help but wonder if she would soon become the same.

"Commander," a voice called. It was a councilor, the young one who had a strange habit of projecting his voice from under his collar. He kept Iphigenia's pace as he delivered some message that was too soft for Mirari to hear.

"Oh, I see," Iphigenia blinked. "At your command, Your Grace." Adder didn't waste a second and galloped to the next commander. From behind, Mirari heard Region Leader Ahden put up some resistance.

"By the soggy oats of—" Ahden said. His whine was followed by silence while he absorbed whatever Adder was saying to him. "Fine, fine. You owe me one."

Adder rode back up to the front, where Fangbane, Starlight, and Councilor Suzan were waiting on the sideline as the soldiers marched forward. Adder said, "They're ready to depart when you are."

"Wonderful," Fangbane said. "My gratitude. Had I told them myself, I'm sure they wouldn't have listened." He then gestured to Suzan. "Your Grace, I leave the main force with you and Councilor Adder. I trust you two know the terrain well enough to set up a barricade at Ganmali."

"Play it safe," Suzan said. "Gaven – he's no kid to mess with."

"Trained by you, I expect no less."

As they left, a fraction of the soldiers had broken off from the main line. While most large carriages and foot soldiers stayed on the path, a small cavalry was waiting for Fangbane's command. Ahden and Erel strode up to him with a handful of cavalry units. Among them were Iphigenia, who was assigned to Erel's team, and Mirari and Joachim, who stopped with the group out of curiosity.

"Good," Fangbane said. "You're coming with us too."

"To... where?" Mirari asked.

"To catch a tiger."

FANGBANE GALLOPED AHEAD of the rest of the party. Along the way, they met with two scouts who reported seeing a mob camping along the banks of Fox River in a narrow, grassy valley of Tilt Forest. They were following a familiar trade route, an easy terrain favored by merchants traveling from Althaea Main to Nanaka.

They arrived at a small hill that overlooked the lower field of Tilt Forest. They were still too far to see Gaven's forces but knew he was within the vicinity.

"In the valley," Erel said as she waved her hand over the vista. "We can surround the southern forest, and they'll have no option but to cross the river. The river will slow them down, and it is bound to cause some confusion."

Fangbane nodded in approval. "I like it."

"Pardon the intrusion," Ahden said as he eased in between Erel and Fangbane. "But do we really have to capture him alive? It'll be a lot quicker if we just put a blade through him."

"So you can take his territory, is that it?" Erel scoffed.

"I'm just considering what you're saying, Lady Erel. If what you say is true, that Gaven is possessed, can he be saved? Would the effort be... worth it?"

Mirari, who had been eavesdropping on the commanders, butted in to their conversation.

"Why not?" she said without a second thought. "He's innocent until the Council rules otherwise."

"What's in it for you, featherpit?" Ahden taunted with a grin that said her remarks only riled him up. "Why are you obsessing over saving an Althaean region leader?"

He had caught her tongue. Mirari, now afraid to say anymore, shrunk away in silence.

"Leave the girl alone." Erel nudged him away, and they continued making her argument to him on the side.

Fangbane cleared his throat and turned to Mirari.

"I know what you're thinking, and no, you will not fight," he said.

Mirari furrowed her brow. "And why not?"

"You are to stay with me, with the command and control team."

"I don't recall agreeing to this."

Fangbane sighed. "Mirari, you are a volunteer in this force. As such, you are subject to my command." He saw an angry, almost defiant look on Mirari's face. "I understand you want to go on this raid, but—"

"I can go with Iffy—"

"No. This is going to be a clash, slash, and withdraw. Even if you walked right up to him, you'd probably be dead before you could open your mouth." He paused as Starlight and Joachim trotted their horses next to them.

"Now, now, let's not jump to conclusions." Starlight said and smiled at Mirari. "Sorren wanted her to come, so there must be a reason."

"Wish he could stop beating around the bush."

"C'mon now. It's not spelled out for him either."

"Where is he now?" Mirari said.

"Observing from the base. Never did enjoy the battlefield. Too much… reading, if I may. I hope you can keep mum about it. He doesn't like people knowing."

Mirari nodded. His ability, Mirari figured, must be some form of clairvoyance. She would have been thrilled to have an ability like that. The other fighters in this party must also have extraordinary powers, levels of kore beyond imagination. All Mirari could offer was her words, and she hoped that was all she needed.

"Our destinies are ever-shifting, depending on the choices we make," Starlight said. "Sorren has advised us to keep you close but out of battle. We can't stop you, Miss Mirari, but his advice always guides us toward the most favorable outcome."

"Miss Mirari," Joachim whispered into Mirari's ear. "I believe they have a point. You must leave the fight to the trained. You have proven yourself useful strategically. Trust the others to do their part of the job."

But she didn't trust them. This light brigade was made up of Althaeans, and she knew they were raised to only one end – to slaughter.

"I will give you a chance to speak to him," Fangbane said. "I promise. Now's just not the time."

Before she could counter both of them, Starlight said, "Ah!

82

This looks like a good spot to set up, don't you think?" She gestured over to an open area, flat land surrounded by large boulders. "May the medics set up here?"

"That looks safe," Fangbane said. He turned back to Mirari. "Mirari, Joachim, can you help her set up?"

Joachim nudged her. "C'mon now."

Mirari wanted to refuse, but Starlight's words stuck in her mind. She knew nothing about how a battlefield worked, much less of the terrains that surrounded them. If she could not fight, then what was her purpose in this brigade? Not in the medical tents, she hoped. But until they found Gaven, she would have to play the game of patience.

OUTSIDE OF THE tent Mirari had helped assemble, she looked up at the night sky. She didn't bother to consult a timepiece – she could read the position of the moon and stars better than any seafaring man, able to navigate not only in space but to tell the time from the sky's movement. She had forced herself to learn ever since her ignorance of the sky almost cost her life. She wanted to study the constellations as well, but since she had to sleep early to rise for morning trading at Solarin, she hadn't gotten to see the stars as much as back when she was a child in Malino.

Starlight seemed to have taken note of her stargazing.

"Do you know how to read them?" Starlight asked. She pointed to a string of bright stars in the west. "You see that box? That's Cordelia's ship. She is with us tonight. And the bird above her... that's Cygnus, the Goddess of Fate."

"And what does that mean?" Mirari asked, now curious.

"We don't know," Starlight said. "Cygnus is... perhaps the most mysterious of all the gods." But despite the eerie warning,

Starlight continued to smile. "We never truly know what she wants. That's how fate works."

"It's a good sign," a voice called. Erel – the woman who ruled by Gaven's side. Mirari wondered what they were like when they worked together. What was their relationship like? Did he have feelings for this woman? She felt compelled to respect her as much as she respected Gaven.

"When you don't see Lachess' constellation next to hers, it's a good sign," Erel explained. She continued in a more spiteful tone, "But good and bad are subjective, aren't they?"

"Ah, Lady Erel," Starlight said, beaming. "So you know the constellations as well?"

"Only the ones that matter." Instead of looking at the lights, Erel's gaze bore into Mirari. Mirari felt a dozen judgments piling on her.

Erel leaned in and took a big whiff of Mirari's hair. Mirari froze, confused and baffled at such strange behavior. She had been riding for days, covered in sweat, hers and the horse's.

Yet Erel said, "You smell nice." Mirari's mouth dropped, unsure of whether or not to take it as a compliment. But her body shivered as Erel's breath tickled her ear and whispered, "But until I know what you are, I don't trust you."

"Lady Erel." Iphigenia waved from the far end. She was accompanied by a few other battle maidens from Oban, beaming with energy no one should have at this late hour. "We're ready for your command."

Erel nodded and pulled away from Mirari. She strapped on a pair of rider's gloves and walked to her team. Iphigenia was under Erel's orders, a move that others would've considered offensive – placing a Minettan commander under an Althaean. But Iphigenia didn't seem bothered by it at all. Though Erel said little, in fact, rarely interacted with any of them at all, Iphigenia gave her full respect to the lady in charge.

"Be safe, Lady Starlight, Miss Mirari," Iphigenia called out. "We'll be back soon."

Erel locked her feet tightly in the stirrup of her gray horse and guided the first cavalry unit with her into the woods. Iphigenia followed with the next group.

They had spotted dozens of campfires burning in the forest. Gaven's forces were estimated in the thousands, whereas they only had a hundred each. But numbers didn't matter. There was no victory to claim. This was a game of stealth.

As Erel rode off into the darkness to confront her traitor of a leader, she couldn't stop thinking of Mirari. It wasn't important right now, but she couldn't take her mind off how such a lovely girl shared something in common with her current enemy.

Erel seethed. Mirari was another one. That made it three people she couldn't copy.

The idea sent her head boiling faster than her heart was racing. Were they related? Was it a coincidence? She couldn't stop pondering over the mystery.

CHAPTER ELEVEN

As Gaven's column got closer to the edge of Tilt Forest, the road widened into a small valley next to Fox River. Gaven's scouts reported that the area was sheltered by thick forests; they could lay invisible to scouts for miles, and tomorrow they would arrive in Ganmali.

"We'll rest here for the night," Gaven said to one of his commanders, Eoin the Blacksmith, a huge man covered with a dozen burn scars across his muscles. He and the rest of the appointed leaders, each leading a group of five hundred or so, were a cadre of radical firebrands who never missed the chance to rouse peasants with grandiose promises of new world order – a world where the common man would control his own destiny and have a say in what their leaders did. These were ideas that Gaven always had sympathy for. But now, he took ideology to the extreme. He burned with a desire to kill any person from any empire who tried to stand in his way.

He had close to two thousand revolutionaries following his lead, most of whom had followed him from Rhea. Some he picked up along the way from small villages, and many more were to join him at Ganmali. The majority were peasant farmers and miners of Althaea Main, but he had no shortage of bakers, artists, and seamstresses that were equally valuable. These strangers defended and supported each other in a time when such a display of kindness would've been considered bizarre. Only a few times did the commanders have to break up petty fights over water and weapons, but there were even more times when Gaven saw the people share their rations with one another, supply each other with blankets, and share cheap entertainment of cards and rocks. His people assembled sticks and long blankets for shelter. Women huddled in circles around campfires, and men were sent to gather wood or prepare weapons.

Eoin jumped to his feet as Gaven patrolled the vicinity. He saluted. "All quiet, Your Honor."

Just seeing the mighty warrior walk among them raised the spirits of the commoners who made up his rebel army. Nobody was going to fall asleep on watch, not with the Valiant Tiger among them.

Gaven nodded and stared into the night. He walked another circuit of his encampment. Something was making him uneasy. He toured the listening posts, checking with the sentries, yet nobody reported seeing or hearing anything.

Eoin watched Gaven as he stood silent, boring a hole into the blackness with a fixed, steady gaze. "Is something wrong, Your Honor?"

The question seemed to jerk Gaven out of a trance-like state. He chewed over his answer, grasping at something.

"So much…" he said. "More than any of us knows…"

Eoin shook his head. He never knew the region leader was such an absent-minded person.

"Your Honor," Eoin began. "If this is a success, if we get the weapons at Ganmali, cross to Valenia, fight off anyone who stands in our way for, I don't know, years to come… what then? What's in it for you, I mean? We fail, you'll lose your head. We succeed, you'll eventually be overthrown. Doesn't matter if you're on our side, Your Honor. In our future, there will be no more region leaders."

"For me…" Gaven hummed, his gaze still fixed on the dark. "I will protect my people… and everyone… who cannot protect themselves." Eoin looked into the forest. Nothing.

But Gaven saw figures, silhouettes with blurred faces.

There was a middle-aged woman, one of those worn and broken mothers who looked like she never knew rest. Her hair was tied in a braid underneath a wool blanket with patches of fabric covering what were once holes. She stood still and stared at him. Not a word came out of her mouth; she simply turned and faded into the dark.

You're going to leave us like she left you?

Gaven heard a familiar male voice, one that annoyed him beyond words. He turned to his left and came across the mischievous noble that was once his partner.

Think about all those people you could've helped, all those soldiers you threw out as bait. You think they'll ever forgive you for that, Gaven?

Then a young girl said, *Was it worth it?*

He peered down and saw the little mistress, half his height. She caressed a purple stone in her palms and showed it to him.

You said you would return it, and you lied. You used us too. How could you?

Gaven's voice was silenced by a knot in his throat. He felt the guilt eating away at his mind. His soul ached, and he wanted to scream for help.

Redeem yourself, Gaven, the male voice said, offering him his palm. *It's the only way for you to be forgiven.*

He stared at the hand with an uneasy temptation. Reaching for the spirit's hand was one of the last things Gaven wanted to do, but it was all he could think of. His body had long disobeyed him, and he was once again falling into the pit, thoughts spiraling into taking the blame for everything that was happening.

He wanted to set things right.

Gaven stepped forward, walking through the transparent girl, feet dragging with every slow step. He signed the demon's contract, ready to do whatever it took to be back in control. His guilt prevented him from turning to face the girl he left behind, but still, he managed to whisper, "I'm sorry, Roselyn."

Gaven stepped beyond his sentry line and walked into the pitch black. The puzzled blacksmith stared at him until he was out of sight. He shrugged, resuming his posted position.

The deeper Gaven moved into the dense forest, away from his camp, the darker it grew. He crept slowly, his senses on alert. He felt the odd confusion in his mind more strongly now, perhaps because the quiet and darkness did not provide any sensory input. The silent blackness left him alone with only the commanding voices in his head.

He stopped after walking for some time, the sounds of his camp far behind. Whatever had been nagging at him, drawing him off into the darkness, he couldn't feel it anymore. He had no motive to be here. The disturbance was gone.

But something, a feeling – one that wasn't quite his own – told him to keep going, a little farther into the woods. It was almost a sixth sense, but it compelled and motivated him, even if he didn't understand the reason for it. He felt no desire to resist these feelings.

After only ten more slow, silent paces, he caught a tiny wink of light. He took a step forward, and it was gone. After three slow, careful steps, he saw it again and stopped. He swayed, leaning from side to side. Unless he was in just the right orientation, he couldn't see the mysterious orange glow. He began to move toward the light, careful not to stray outside the line of sight of the twinkling beam.

When he was close enough to confirm that the light was coming from a campfire, his warrior senses kicked into high gear. This source, whoever lit this fire, was not from his army.

Gaven held his spear in hand as he assessed the encampment.

Two people were sitting by the fire, a man and a woman, with guards to their right. He was too far to make out a face, but he recognized the man's blue cloak that bore the winged emblem of Axillaire.

Gaven couldn't believe the region leader bothered to intervene in his rebellion. But reinforcements coming from other regions was one piece of intel out of many his scouts had picked up. He had known Ahden for years. Hunted with him, drank with him, even considered him a close ally despite his rough competitive spirit.

And yet, Gaven felt no affection for him now – just a need to get him out of the way.

But this camp was too small to be Ahden's entire army – figuring by the number of tents, which was no more than a dozen. And most of these troops weren't even here – just a skeleton reserve force, it appeared. He knew this was not like Ahden's strategy at all; he liked to travel with at least a thousand men by his side and set up his quarters close to the culinary. He would mingle with at least a dozen ladies he brought along with a drink in hand. Here, it was a single woman.

Gaven knew there must be someone else leading him. His scouts also reported hearing that fighters across the alliance had gathered a massive army to come after the rebels. He thought it was too good to be true and, quite frankly, too ambitious of a task. To convince all three empires to stick their nose in Althaea's revolution? Every fighter and politician knew that was an impossible ideology. Still, Gaven kept that possibility in mind, knowing to never underestimate his opponents.

CHAPTER TWELVE

E rel and Iphigenia lined their soldiers along the outskirts of the valley. After fording Fox River, Erel had her cavalry troops dismount.

"On foot," she ordered. "And I will strangle any soldier who makes a sound." But she knew it wouldn't be necessary. These were some of Oban's most skilled fighters, the best in all of Minetta. Iphigenia had lent Valkyries from her army after Erel suffered huge casualties at the battle of Rhea. With Haynes still recovering from his injuries, Erel was commanding alone.

Even without Erel's guidance, the soldiers had wrapped every metal buckle and clasp with cloth to assure not a single clank or jingle would be heard when they infiltrated the rebel base. These Valkyries were trained well – too clever to be mere soldiers – and complete opposites of the recruits raised in Althaea Main. Few women joined the army in Althaea, and as a result, Erel had to deal with men – difficult creatures whose egos and pride surpassed their common sense. She started to regret that her younger self did not seek refuge in Oban instead.

Iphigenia's forces crept from the south, moving through the

trees like wraiths. They took their positions and waited for Erel's signal to attack.

———

MEANWHILE AT THE CAMP, Ahden set down a jug of beer on a log and took a seat. He patted the empty space next to him. "Why don't you tell me why you're really here, darling."

"I humbly refuse," Mirari said, her arms remaining folded across her chest. She had nowhere to go. Erel and Iphigenia had taken off, and Starlight left her in charge of watching the supplies while she went with other healers to collect herbs. Joachim was keeping watch on the other side of the tents, some ways out of her sight. She was stuck here with Ahden, whose division wasn't scheduled to attack until Erel's unit returned.

"You remind me of someone, you know?" He took a large sip of his beer. "It's... kind of taboo to talk about it these days, but I think we should, in her memory. She was young and beautiful, an ocean of silk hair, dimples like the sun, and eyes... well, those emeralds shined brighter than the diamonds on my coat."

She rolled her eyes. "Why are you telling me this?"

"She didn't know when to give up. Stubborn, just like you. And that cost her life in battle."

Mirari turned to him. "You calling me stupid?"

"Arrogantly daft. You're no fighter. No fancy sword is going to make up for your aura that reeks like last season's cod. I'm telling you, don't fight a battle you can't win." He took another sip of his beer. Mirari was convinced it wasn't his first jug. Ahden started at the crackling of firewood in front of him. "But..." he continued with a deep sigh, "I'm willing to bet every case of beer in this camp that if I could ask that maiden now, there's nothing she would've done differently that day. Nothing. She wouldn't have regretted losing her life to save the people she loved. You seem to be doing the same."

Mirari chuckled. "I'm not doing anything like that."

"No? So why are you here? To cheer us on?"

Turning away, she said, "I have my reasons."

"That old umbra with you is your retainer, correct? So, what noble house are you from?"

"I'm... not a noble," she lied.

"Then I suppose you're just a wealthy peasant," he said. "Fair enough. Who am I to care? That's none of my business. We're just having a chat now, is all."

"And you're prying, Your Honor."

"But I'm not wrong, am I?" He grinned as he clinked his mug against her full glass before chugging the liquid down to the last drop. He let out a satisfying *ahh*. "I'm never wrong."

A wry smile etched the corner of her lips. How different would this all have turned out if she just admitted that she was a Hale? If she supplied this rescue operation with her family's inventions? Would she have power over all these honored fighters? Would she have a bigger say in what happened to Gaven?

But once she lifted that chilled cup to her lips and savored the bitter taste trickling down her throat, she knew she wouldn't give up this moment. A night under the stars, on a dangerous venture into the unknown, and something so simple as a cold, refreshing glass of beer.

This freedom wasn't possible as a noble; those fancy scrooges refrained from consuming a commoner's drink, only fancied wine and aged cheese. To sleep on raw earth where the smallest kick in the mud could ruin your silk dress? Out of the question. And with all the duties that came with being a Hale, overseeing operations over several regions and spending weeks on business negotiations, there would be no time to be in the company of strangers.

And even though Ahden was a region leader from a rival empire and a misogynistic scum that knew no boundaries, Mirari enjoyed hearing his stories and his strange way of cheering her on. He was taunting her but also giving praise.

Ahden stopped short of reaching for another glass. He noticed the rustle of leaves that didn't flow with the harmonic wind.

Something hacked past the two Axillarian foot soldiers on his right before either of them could shout an alarm or draw their swords. He reached for a metal stick in his back pocket, no bigger than an arrowhead, and swung it around.

Mirari heard a clang but saw nothing except flying sparks of metal upon impact.

In the blink of an eye, Ahden had kicked their jugs to the ground and leapt over the log bench. His stick extended left and right into a long spear, and he struck at an intruder only inches from his face.

Mirari barely saw his opponent in the faint illumination from their campfire – a stalwart warrior with his glowing spear. He was tall, at least six feet, and from her angle, she could make out his cyan eyes. If she reached out her hand, she would be able to touch his chest. And she wanted to – there was something familiar and protective about him that dissipated all the dangers she should've felt.

Suddenly, she was yanked to the side, away from the two men sealed in glares. Joachim had two daggers out, ready to join the fight.

"Are you hurt, Milady?" Joachim asked. Mirari shook her head. The two warriors were locked in combat, a fight that would soon turn deadly. "We should leave," Joachim said.

But oblivious to the dangers of the duel, Mirari wanted to stay and help if she could. She stood still, refusing to move, leaving Joachim no choice but to wait and watch it unfold with her.

The intruder took a few steps to the side, and Ahden followed his footwork in the opposite direction. They traced a circle around the campfire like a Viscarian tribal dance, spears up and chests out as if a string was pulling them together. Ahden mirrored his opponent's pace. A game of patience. A test of rhythm. Now it was a matter to see who would strike first.

When the warrior got close enough to the light of the fire, Mirari could see the dragon emblem waving on his cerulean cape, now slashed in black ink and replaced with a circular crest she had never seen before. His eyes were lit by the dancing flames, radiating like turquoise and cyan stones in a freshwater stream.

"Would you like the chance to explain yourself, Gaven?" Ahden said, keeping his eyes locked on Gaven's.

Mirari gasped as his name took her breath away.

In a tone duller than unsweetened kippin tea, he responded, "You're in my way."

"Tch. Of course."

Gaven responded by lunging, which Ahden blocked with a quick swipe of his pole. Gaven's spear bounced back, deflected off nothing. At least, nothing he could see.

Mirari didn't recognize him. The scrawny farm boy she once knew had been replaced by this chiseled warrior, full of resolve and adversity. She couldn't imagine what he had gone through since she had last seen him. He moved as if he was familiar with taking blood time after time. He had truly become one of them – relentless, blood-thirsty Althaeans who engaged in murder for entertainment.

But Mirari wanted to believe that the person she knew was still there. Now was her chance, but she didn't know what to say. She felt the pressure of time, frantic to take action before the men killed each other.

Gaven took swing after swing, each bouncing off of the shaft of Ahden's pole. He was able to knock it upward and away from its master. When it fell and lodged into the dirt, it was only half of the spear, which now stuck out like a dagger with a tail of glowing kore. It pulled itself out, hovering over the dirt, before returning to the chipped end of Ahden's spear.

Mirari's mouth dropped. She knew her family had developed kore weapons that could follow their owners' commands, but they were all stars and daggers, weapons used by umbras. She didn't know there were spears that could do the same, and certainly not a spear that could split into two.

Ahden was a warrior with more skill than strength, and that sneaky weapon worked well with his cunning style. But Gaven had seen it before.

It was decades ago, long before Gaven joined the Althaean army, when Ahden was known as a conqueror, a thirsty fighter always out to seize as many territories as possible. At the age of eighteen, he defeated the region leader of Nanaka in a duel and took the throne. It hardly satisfied his thirst for power. Only a few years later, he went to seek a larger prize – the region of Axillaire, the border to Valenia. He claimed it with much ease and little criticism, for the people knew there was no one better to defend the border than this young prodigy.

When Gaven became commander, Stein invited this legend to duel with his "nephew," not for his territory but as entertainment for their advisors and commanders. Gaven had studied Ahden's style, the way he liked to confuse his opponents in a masterful dance of swords and play with his prey before a feast. Once Gaven learned his ways, half a dozen duels later, he was able to take a victory swing.

And now, Gaven intended to do the same.

Soldiers began to emerge from their tents, circling the camp with Fangbane. But before they could get in range of him, Gaven raised his hand. A wall of earth rose around the camp, enclosing the duel in a ten-foot-high wall sturdy as thousand-year-old cliffs, separating Mirari, Joachim, and Ahden from the rescue team.

"Mirari!" She could hear Fangbane scream from the other side, followed by sounds of pounding against the thick walls.

"I'm ok," she reassured him.

"I know what you're thinking, and don't you dare. Stay away from him."

"I can talk to him."

"He could kill you."

But Mirari didn't care. It would hurt her more if she didn't try. The sight of him brought her no fear.

"Joachim," Fangbane called out, knowing there was little he could do from the other side of the wall. "Don't let her do anything stupid."

"On my life, sir," Joachim promised, then saw that Mirari was easing her way into the fight, one careful step after another with nothing but raised bare hands. He observed patiently.

CLASH, slash, block – the two region leaders locked spears, their grim and gritty faces just inches apart, pushing spear against spear with all their strength.

The top end of Ahden's spear popped off, the sharp point aimed at Gaven. One glare was all it took for the ground under their feet to shoot up. A large stone, thin as a tablet, acted like a shield on Gaven's side. It deflected the dagger, then launched at Ahden's head.

Ahden fumbled, but not before the two ends of his spear boomeranged back to his opponent. Gaven twirled his spear in a flourish, swinging left and right as the spear ends curved back to him over and over again. Each strike came at full force, propelled by the strength of controlled wind surrounding their trajectory. But at the right angle, Gaven drove the blades into his earthy walls, lodged in too tight for it to pull out on its own.

"Joachim," Mirari yelled as she lunged forward. "Restrain him, now!"

Her shout distracted Gaven. He saw the young lady, who had

been standing on the sideline, now charging at him. As he took a step forward, ready to counter her, he tripped over a small piece of raised earth. It hadn't been there before, and it was too small for Gaven to take notice.

When he lost his balance, Joachim dashed to Gaven's side, and with the snap of his cowhide whip, lightning stings coiled around Gaven's arms. Gaven fell to the side, arms confined and raised in the air by the sturdy whip.

Mirari was in between him and Ahden now, arms wide to protect her comrade.

Gaven's eyes drew to the spear that lay between him and the maiden. He could break free and take the spear if he wanted to – the whip binding his arms was but paper to him. Even the man who had confined him was no match. He knew he could take down all three of them if he was given five minutes and leave with barely a scratch. But he didn't have five minutes to spare. The overwhelming numbers on the other side would break his wall long before then.

He forced his attention on the young lady, petite and curled into her insecurities. In contrast to Ahden, her aura was so faint that he assumed she was just a woman for Ahden's entertainment.

But her bravery caught his attention. He didn't know her, yet her eyes were speaking, trying to tell him something... but what?

He examined her physique and analyzed her level of threat, which was close to none. She was armed, at least, a fine-looking sword hung at her hip. But her hands were empty, and she was holding them out before her in a gesture of peace and friendship.

"What are you doing, Gav?" She spoke in a sweet melody that he hadn't heard for many years, and she leaned in a little closer to get a better look at his face.

"Careful, Milady," Joachim whispered, his hands trembling and knuckles turning white from his strong grip on the whip, but she kept inching forward.

Gaven could only look at her as if she was crazy for approaching him. But he sensed that she was not afraid. She stayed calm and at peace, projecting a gentle aura that blanketed his own aggressive thirst for blood.

"Gaven?" she probed. Her eyes – deep pools of purple, kind, and almost... familiar – entranced him, and he was unable to look away. "If you keep doing this, they're going to kill you," she said. "You didn't work this hard to end up like this. I know it. So can you... please surrender?"

Gaven heard two knives cut through the wind. He stayed frozen, letting the sound scratch his ear. He tilted his head slightly to the side, barely dodging the blades. He tore free like a gorilla, stomping, building up a geyser of dirt to waylay Joachim. The whip around his wrist loosened, and he reached for the spear by his feet. Ahden's blades were whirling back, and Gaven swiped them away. The blades clanged on the floor, then levitated off the ground, returning to the owner's side. Gaven's attention was on Ahden, who was now back on his feet.

"You're crazy, woman!" Ahden shouted, with both his hovering daggers behind him, ready to take another strike.

"Your Honor, stop!" Mirari begged. But the two men were immersed in battle, and she no longer had their attention. Joachim, landing back on his feet, pulled Mirari away from the action.

The waving daggers clawed at Gaven in a fury, swinging from all directions, left and right. But Gaven could see it all, deflecting each hit. One dagger left a cut down his sleeve. The scratch distracted him, and he missed the incoming hit of the other dagger, which lodged into his left shoulder and forced him to drop his weapon.

Gaven groaned and tried to yank it out. The dagger was coming at him too fast, and he saw his inevitable fate.

Clang!

A sword intercepted the dagger aimed at his chest, batting it away like a game of buttonball. And much to both men's surprise, it was the lady who had taken the swing.

Ahden hissed, "Seriously?"

"You can't kill him," Mirari said. "Those are the orders."

"Close to dead still counts."

But Mirari ignored Ahden and faced Gaven once again. She dropped her sword and placed both her hands on his shoulder. "Come on, Gav. Please stop this before he kills you."

As mental as this woman was, Gaven thought, she had full confidence in what she was doing. Her presence brought him a sense of comfort and familiarity, kindling a dying flame that had been taking shelter under thin debris.

Ahden yielded, seeing that her words had some effect. He waited.

"You remember me, don't you?" Mirari asked.

Gaven stayed stiff, like a doll. Her sweet words were like a harmony sweeping into Gaven's dark mind. And when she spoke, it overshadowed all the other figures plaguing his thoughts.

"I'm the one who always ate your beans when Sal wasn't looking. The one who would put bitterworms down your shirt." Mirari waited, searching in his eyes for a sign of hope. In desperation, she spoke the name she had hoped she'd never use again. "Roselyn... D-Do you remember Roselyn?"

Gaven opened his mouth slightly, wanting to speak, but he couldn't pull past that knot in his throat. The tug in his chest lowered him, transporting him away from the light and drowning him in shadowy waters. Whispers stung his ear. He groaned and began to scream.

Take revenge.

Redeem yourself.

Kill her.

Desperate to make those voices stop, he raised his spear, ready to take a blow at the shadow figure before him.

Mirari gasped, but she didn't yield. She stared, waiting,

perhaps wondering if he was really going to strike. Then she shrieked, closing her eyes as she saw the swift movement of his arm crashing down.

There was a warm splatter upon her face where there should've been pain... and immediately she opened her eyes.

His bright spear had run through the Region Leader of Axillaire. The other end poked out through his abdomen, and Ahden dropped to his knees.

Gaven's vision focused, even sharpened, as he was drawn to the fresh blood dripping from his blade. The blood captivated him – he stared at it in a state of rapture. It ran in rivulets, dripping down the hard steel. He focused on a single drop, rolling down the edge of the blade like a human life running out onto the earth.

He wondered why he was doing this. But over and over again the voices in his mind told him...

Because only you can do what's right.

Joachim held a blade at Gaven's throat. The warrior didn't resist. He was lost, knowing what he had done.

"So the rumors of possession are true," Joachim said, seeing Gaven's hollow expression. "And there's still some human left in you." Gaven didn't respond or budge, but Joachim remained cautious. If he lowered the blade, Gaven could take him out with a quick elbow. Joachim didn't have a good angle to reach for his whip or to secure Gaven's hands. He could only wait.

Meanwhile, Mirari held Ahden in her arms and looked over his wound. The spear was still lodged through his abdomen, and Mirari was hesitant to pull it out. She was no healer and was essentially useless in this situation. Still, she wanted to comfort him in honor of his sacrifice.

"Just... just stay calm, okay," Mirari stuttered as she looked around for something to use. She had no renastōnes, no healing kore; she could only offer him her words. The pounds against the earthy wall, which had now begun to crack and crumble, synchronized with the thumps of her heart.

"I think you're the one who needs to calm down... Milady," Ahden wheezed through his weakened breath.

"H-How do I stop the bleeding?" Mirari asked. "What do I do?"

"Shhh." He had a mischievous grin on his face despite being in excruciating pain. "I know why you're here."

"Now may not be the time for that."

"I know that feeling more than anyone in this empire. You look up to him. He doesn't need you. But still, you'd take a blade for him... The crazy things we do for family."

Mirari stayed quiet. Gaven's Minettan origin wasn't something she should be telling a stranger. But how much longer was he going to hold out? Was this the time to be worried about politics? Before her was a fighter, a human much like any other soldier, regardless of the cape color they wore.

"I'm sorry," Mirari said. If he died, it would be on her for failing to stop Gaven, trying to prove that he wasn't violent at the cost of many lives, and failing to help or heal the injured leader in her arms.

"I was wrong," Ahden snickered, followed by a cough of blood. "He listens to you. Gaven's a handful, but if anyone can save that fool, it will be you."

An explosion sent rocks flying, leaving a hole in the massive wall. Fangbane and Starlight rushed out and caught sight of Mirari and Ahden, and Joachim with his blade at Gaven's neck.

Gaven snarled upon seeing the number of reinforcements before him, and with a heavy grunt, he pulsed out a barrier strong enough to knock Joachim off his feet.

Then Gaven took off, long before Joachim got back to his feet. Fangbane and Starlight rushed to their sides. Dozens of men behind them were on standby, spears and swords out.

"Are you alright?" Fangbane asked as he patted and examined Mirari like a child who had fallen off a swing. Mirari didn't know what to say. Adrenaline was rushing through her, yet her mind was hollow.

"Darling…" he heard Starlight gasp. Fangbane turned to his wife. Starlight, Ridge, and a few other healers were standing over a pool of blood staining the earth.

Ridge took a look at Ahden, and her expression flushed with fear. She had her hands over her mouth, trying to hold back a wail. She swallowed her desire to scream. She inhaled, then focused her spiritual energy into her palms. She unraveled a green renastōne from her pocket. The yellow veins in the stone lit up and illuminated over Ahden's wound. Starlight's hands gripped onto the handle of the spear lodged in his abdomen, ready to pull it out on Ridge's command.

"Ahden…" Fangbane shook his head, but the headstrong Althaean hadn't given up yet.

He turned his head slightly, grinning his playful grin. With his last strength, he mouthed to Fangbane and Mirari, "Go get him."

CHAPTER THIRTEEN

G aven rubbed his heels raw, crashing wildly back into the woods the way he came. He ignored the slapping branches and leapt over fallen logs. He had to join his men and prepare them for battle. The firelight ahead grew brighter, and the song of battle rose to a crescendo.

When he drew closer, he realized the light hadn't come from their campfire. Their tents had been set aflame.

The men in the vanguard, the best fighters under his command, ran in chaotic directions. He had only a few ex-military officers among his thousands of rebels and a handful of non-commissioned sergeants who knew what they were doing. The troops that would have been the first to charge into battle bumbled about in disorganized panic, half asleep and in terror.

He dashed into the chaos, shoving, hollering, ordering his men to arm themselves. He grabbed a young bugler by the collar.

"Call assembly. Now! We have to mount a counterattack," he said, slapping, shaking, and screaming at the few experienced officers in his motley horde.

The rest stumbled around like ants from a kicked-over

anthill. Some had retreated into the waters, frantic to reach the other side. The stream was no more than knee deep but ran with a strong current. Wading across was a slow, exhausting business. Along the way, they were met with arrows and bear traps lying in the waters while enemy forces waited on the other side.

IPHIGENIA'S FOOT soldiers cut them down like weeds once they reached the other side of the steam, and their blood spattered the air like the floating seeds of dandelions. She waded into the melee, the smooth mechanics of her perfectly trained sword work spilling blood with cold, deadly efficiency.

On the outskirts of the valley, Erel took pleasure in seeing the rebels panic. Her first line, the troops that stirred up the chaos, came back without a casualty. They waited until the last of Iphigenia's troops pulled out, then Erel's forces moved back in.

The rebel's sentry line didn't have time to give out an alarm, as the sound of thundering hooves was all around them. Erel's cavalry swarmed them with spears and swords, cutting them down.

She saw her combatants facing only token resistance. They could keep going, hacking until the last of the rebels surrendered. They could swiftly kill fifty, a hundred, maybe more. And she wanted to, but by that time, the entire army of rebels would be aroused. She knew her troops must fall back before that, while escape was still easy.

Sting like bees, then fly away; that was their plan.

Running away was not Erel's style, nor was it of her soldiers, but to make Fangbane's strategy work, she knew she had to obey.

Erel pulled her forces out as Iphigenia's Valkyries ran back in. As she trotted to lay still in the dark parts of the forest, she saw a numbskull dashing in the opposite direction of the rebel's retreat.

Once she got a good look at him, it all made sense – it was her former leader.

The sight hit like a blow to her chest. She watched him rally a heavy battle cry as he charged into Iphigenia's cavalry units. He hacked and slashed at anything in his way, not acknowledging the brave fighters who dared to cross his path even for a second.

Erel galloped over to a dark patch of land where she knew Iffy would be positioned. She found Iphigenia pulling out her sword from the leg of a dead man and flicking off the blood from her blade. She was so calm as if she was plucking fresh flowers from the field. The sight of blood and death didn't bother her in the slightest. She was not at all what Erel expected.

"Retreat," Erel ordered. "This raid is over."

"What?" Iphigenia was stunned. "Is it not working?"

"The Valiant Tiger is hacking his way through your line. This is no longer your battle."

"What do you mean? This is *our* battle."

"I will finish what I failed to do," Erel shouted. "But I will not let you get involved. Take your Valkyries back to camp and inform them of the situation." She snapped the reins and shouted, "Forward!"

Erel weaved through Iphigenia's soldiers, leaving behind the rest of the Valkyries that were temporarily in her command. Only the original soldiers from Althaea Main followed Erel and charged at their commander to finish what they started.

"Lady Erel!" Iphigenia cried back, but it was no use.

Erel charged into the bright cluster of engulfed rebel tents, swinging her sword like a reaper bringing in a good harvest. Half of the rebels who stumbled out of their tents weren't even armed. Behind her, her Althaean brawlers swung deadly arcs with long-handled hammers, cracking skulls like an Eudoxian polo player. Her cavalry took up their battle cry, but the panicked screams drowned out their war cries.

She charged straight for Gaven. Her horse took a grand leap

over fallen soldiers, and her sword came crashing down on the Valiant Tiger.

He saw the incoming commander flying on her mount and raised his spear. A loud clang boomed through the forest, and he stumbled farther back than he expected. When he looked up, he realized why.

The tiny rider was replaced by a stout, bearded commander with arms as mighty as anvils. He boomed in a husky voice, "Who are you? And what have you done with our leader?"

Gaven looked at Erel with interest, almost as if he didn't dare to kill the rare specimen. She could transform into the legendary brawler who lifted Lake Urabe, and his skill could outmatch hers. But her creative intelligence? He may not be able to keep up.

"You... have strong resolve, Erel," Gaven said. "I always envied that about you."

She charged at him again, lunging into another stab. He pivoted his horse just enough to avoid her blade. When he turned back, her horse no longer had a rider. She had reached for an upper branch, now taking form as a tiny child, nimble as a monkey. She swayed and fell forward. On her way down, she grew tenfold, and slammed straight into Gaven with the strength of five horses kicking.

If it had been any other human, they would've been flattened, skull cracked on impact. But as dust flew upward, her body only left a large crater in the ground, with Gaven secure in a transparent dome of kore that he held up with both hands.

He dropped his shield and launched his feet into the air. Along the way, head-sized rocks ejected upward from the ground, and he kicked two heavy rocks at her. Then three more. They slammed into her and shattered like dry biscuits, doing no more than tickling her skin. But her movements were sluggish, too slow to block Gaven's mighty kick that sent her tumbling on her back like a helpless turtle. She hissed, her hand clutching her abdomen as she struggled to concentrate. Her body was forced into her normal form — a taller, skinner frame with a cascade of lime-colored hair and radiant golden eyes.

A strange gust picked up in the otherwise still night. The trees did not sway, nor did the leaves flutter. Yet, this gale was clearly targeting him, circling around his feet.

Gaven turned and saw a large branch – longer than a horse and carriage – carried by strong gusts. It slammed into him. His spear flew from his hand, disappearing into some bush in the dark, and his body was nailed against a tree, now buried among the debris.

Iphigenia dashed toward him, sword out as she waited for Gaven to emerge from under the branch weighing down his body.

"I told you to leave," Erel said, wobbling as she picked herself up. It was the first time in years anyone besides Gaven had seen her true form, but at this point, she didn't care. Her only resolve was to make sure Gaven was put to a halt.

To her surprise, Iphigenia didn't question her new appearance. She wasn't fazed at all to see a shapeshifter.

"Lady Erel," Iphigenia called out. "You will not fight him alone!"

As soon as Gaven emerged from the debris, Iphigenia charged straight at him. Her blade slashed enough to lay a shallow wound. Blood – he saw it, felt it, even tasted it all around him in the mist.

Erel landed a high kick, one that made Gaven stumble. He caught the second advance, swung her overhead and around like the God of Thunder, and hammered her into the ground.

The wind picked up again. This time it swept under his feet and slid him forward as if he was tied to a galloping carriage. He landed several feet away, now at the mercy of the Minettan warrior.

Gaven got to his feet and took a swing with his fist, but Iphigenia dropped and spun so that he half tripped, half crashed into her. She kicked both her legs upward, using the strength in her thighs and his own momentum to hurl Gaven up and forward in a tumbling arc.

As he crashed hard on the forest floor, Erel came up behind him. Only his lightning-fast reflexes spared his limb as he dodged the blade. But still, her blade's edge carved a gash across his side.

Gaven was now up on his feet, hands in front of his face. He had one weapon left in his belt – a bloodied dirk. It was useless trying to block a sword blow with that little needle of a blade.

Erel and Iphigenia kept him locked from both sides. They circled, feigning moves and false jabs. Gaven was at the mercy of their strikes. The more blood he lost, the slower his reflexes got. But he didn't dare look down, not even a slight glance, to see how badly he was wounded.

He slowed his movement just a sliver, trying to time the rate of their jabs. When Iphigenia reached out again, Gaven sandwiched her blade between his hands.

She was bewildered, staring at the maniac before her with red trickling down his hands. He managed to yank the sword from her hands and landed a devastating kick to her chest. Iphigenia crashed into a tree trunk several feet away.

Erel broke into a sprint, transformed into a giant brawler, mid-swing, and tackled him. Erel met the warrior fist to fist, pushing each other and locked in a game of strength. Gaven loosened his grip, let Erel fall forward off-balance, and elbowed her in the abdomen. It was not a regular jab. Gaven had enforced his hit with kore, inflicting pain so great it was as if she fell off the edge of a rocky cliff and landed on a pointed rock.

The pain caused her to retract back into her normal form again. Erel fell to the ground in a fetal position. Gaven pulled the dirk from his belt and raised it over her head.

He waited for a split second – not for Erel, but for her ally in this battle. He counted the sound of her steps. Gaven spun around, and Iphigenia was greeted by the abrupt turn of his blade, now lodged into her chest.

Erel watched helplessly from the cold ground. "Iffy!"

Iphigenia stared at Gaven as her vision darkened and spots danced before her eyes. As weakness washed through her, cold and sleepy, she couldn't hold her arms up any longer. Her hands fell to her side. She was waiting for Gaven to end it – but he was mesmerized at the sight of her blood running. He gaped at the darkening stain spreading across her breasts, down past her belly, soaking her entire tunic, and running down her thighs.

Gaven grasped the hilt of his dirk in hand and gently drew it out. An arterial font of crimson burst from her chest, pulsing with each pounding beat of her heart. Her world was dark now. The sound of her pumping heart began to fade into silence, and when Erel could no longer hear its beating, she knew her world was gone.

Gaven's eyes seemed almost aglow with bloodlust. He scanned with his free hand, feeling the blood seeping freely over his fingers. He brought his hand to his lips and tasted the hot, coppery gore.

Erel felt a shiver of revulsion at seeing him lick his bloody fingers. She erupted in an agonizing scream. "I'll make your blood flow like the Evaleen River itself!"

He looked at her, now with the dirk pointed in her direction.

Before he could hold good on his resolve, his attention was drawn to the sound of horses neighing, and he saw men approaching from all sides. The rest of the light brigade was catching up. His shifting eyes told her he knew better than to engage. With his injuries, he wouldn't be able to fend off the rest of her allies.

Gaven dashed to the nearest mount and kicked it forward without securing himself completely in the saddle.

And though Erel didn't want to let him go, she had to admit defeat.

She looked down at the lifeless body of the young Valkyrie who fought by her side. What she saw was no less than a sister, a comrade who had no reason to die before her time. She wondered if she had listened to Fangbane's orders, perhaps there would've been fewer casualties, fewer injuries, one less sacrifice.

As her soldiers closed in, she inhaled and transformed back into her disguise, the second in command of Althaea Main. Erel still had a rabid leader to catch.

CHAPTER FOURTEEN

The sun was beginning to light the sky, but Gaven would bet all the fortunes in the Althaean Sea that only a few of his people got rest that night. He had forced them to keep moving until they passed the next mountain when he was certain his enemies were no longer tracking them. Gaven posted triple the guards, but almost every man and woman in camp spent the rest of the night awake or tossing in short, fitful bursts of sleep. The mere memory of the assault from the blackness of those cursed woods left the whole rebel army on edge and exhausted. They had three hours of rest at most – with no campfire, few supplies, and many friends lost – until he rallied them to stand up and march again.

"A word with you, Your Honor," Eoin the blacksmith greeted, now with patches taped to his chin and forearm. "We lost a quarter of our men last night. Since we would be unable to take them home to their families, it seems that the least we can do is give the fallen a proper burial."

Gaven stroked his stubbled chin, pausing. "In war, the dead are dead, and the living must keep living. We need to move."

"Move where?" He spoke with the power and bravery no one

else had left. "They know where we are now. There's a high chance they know we'll be after the weapons in Ganmali. If we march there now, we'll be asking to be trapped."

"We can still make it before them." He patted Eoin's shoulder, then continued leading the men at the front. "Move it, people. We're wasting daylight. GO!"

Eoin shook his head and directed his attention to the remaining medics still packing up the blankets and cookware they had left.

"Could you?" he asked the medics. "A short prayer and a hole in the earth. I'll join you." The medics nodded, more than pleased to stay behind. In fact, they weren't the only ones who had begun to lose faith in Gaven's plan. After last night, they weren't sure if the battle was worth fighting anymore.

FANGBANE WAS GIVEN a similar appeal for a burial detail by Kieran. He pushed it as a spiritual necessity. "The Grand Celta Priest will not stand for leaving the worthy, blessed dead out in the open for the crows to feast."

"I'm sorry, Kieran. We can't waste time."

"We have the main troops waiting at Ganmali. What's the rush?"

"We need all hands on deck. Their numbers alone overwhelm us."

But Kieran persisted. "If you do not bury the dead, I will order all the troops the celtas have sent to abandon you."

"It won't matter. By the time the Grand Celta Priest hears of it, we'll have Gaven in hand, and his support will be unnecessary."

"I don't need approval from His Holiness," Kieran said. "He has given me authority to act in the interest of our faith, with the full blessing of Oris at my discretion."

Fangbane already knew this. But he wanted Kieran to put his defiance on the record. "Has he indeed? Then please spell out very discreetly what you are threatening."

"I will have *all* our healers *and* all our troops withdraw from your campaign. We will return to the Tribe of Celtas effective immediately. Is that how you want to be remembered in history? That in your bold pursuit of joining fighters from different empires to fight together, you *ironically* failed to respect different cultures, and hence, it led to the failure of your operation?"

Fangbane could certainly succeed without Kieran's troops. But it was the healers he couldn't afford to lose. Starlight had already emphasized their importance with her concerns over the shortage of resources they had. So he gave in to Kieran – just a little.

"I'll let you have a dozen men for burial, but only on your word that the burials will be fast – no extensive prayers, no elaborate grave markers. The ceremonies can wait until the end of the war. Are we agreed?"

"As long as we get them into the ground and take five minutes to say the lament for the dead, that is fine."

Surveying the bloody aftermath of the night's fighting, Kieran ordered the stronger troops to gather all the dead and bring them to the abandoned patch of ground where Fangbane's team took rest.

When Kieran noticed that they were bringing in only the dead from their own troops, he scowled. "I don't see any rebel bodies. Why not? There are certainly plenty of them out there."

"Rebels, sir?" A soldier scratched at his beard. "You don't expect us to bury them, do you?"

"Their living bodies were at war with the government," said Kieran with genuine solemnity. "Not their eternal souls."

The burly soldier sighed as he went to tell his fellow gravediggers it was going to be a long day.

EOIN and his crew made it back to their camp. After gathering a dozen bodies, he noticed five other men on the far side of the forest doing the same. They had four healers, hunched over piles of dirt and whispering into their palms, all being watched by a scrawny man wearing the long, white silks of celta robes. The blacksmith watched carefully, seeing that three of them were digging graves.

But what struck him was they had gathered both the fallen armored soldiers of the alliance and an even larger pile of peasants from the rebel force.

"Stay here," Eoin said to his men. "If I don't come back in five minutes, make tracks back to the main force." Eoin shouldered the only weapon he carried – a shovel. He marched toward the one officer he could see was in command of the burial detail – simply because he wore a gold-tailored sash and seemingly refused to soil his hands with dirt.

The celta noble took notice of the unfamiliar giant that was approaching him. Through his small, round glasses, he gave him a hostile glare. His hands were laced behind his back, hiding a lightning crystal in his sleeve as he waited to see what the stranger would do.

Eoin raised his arm with the shovel in hand, but instead of striking Kieran, it lodged into the ground in front of him. Though he didn't expect to be handed the gift, Kieran's expression remained unchanged.

"Looks like you could use another one," Eoin said before turning back to his men. Kieran stared at the shovel. In no gods' way was he about to do the work of a peasant, but he admired the shovel for another reason – a symbol of peace and respect for the fallen.

Both sides worked without exchanging any words. They pitched in with the enemy, digging graves, burying men who gave their lives for their beliefs, and saying short, solemn prayers over their hallowed resting ground.

NOT LONG AFTER, Eoin kicked his horse into high gear. His small group was able to catch up with the rest of the rebel army, who were taking one final rest in a prairie caressed between high rocky mountains. To his surprise, the crowd had doubled in size, joined by more supporters of the cause. Those who had suffered from the raid last night were now in the care of others who offered blankets, warm stew, and more medical personnel.

He caught sight of their leader on a ridge between two mountains. Gaven sat comfortably in his saddle, looking across the plain at the gently rolling hills that continued to the foot of the towering peaks beyond.

Eoin rode up to him to see the view for himself. There it was at last – a vista extending beyond a couple of miles of farmland and pastures to buildings of gathering density, crowding together to form a small city.

Northwest of the city stood a massive building of gray stone blocks. It was unadorned and without windows, with sentries visible atop battlements. Guards on horseback patrolled the acres of property, all open ground, surrounding the Ganmali Armory. The building was far more solid than some ordinary warehouse. The weapons stored inside were guarded behind high, thick stone walls and the latest protective wards.

"The scouts said there are three thousand approaching from the north," Gaven said. "First, we'll pinch Ganmali from both sides, then head for the armory. Once that's secured, we'll be able to make the city our safe house."

"And is there really no one here to stop us?" Eoin asked, skeptical of the clear view. The forces that attacked them the night before were nowhere to be seen. And to reach Ganmali, they would need to cross a boulder field, another hour of marching between skyscraping mountains, perfect for enemies to hide. Even though he saw no one, he knew it was too good to be true.

Many of Gaven's men had adrenaline coursing through their veins. They still felt the sting of the surprise attacks last night, and they were spoiling for a chance to make up for it.

CHAPTER FIFTEEN

Mirari rested her head on Joachim's back. With their men and supplies diminished, all was quiet, besides the clicks and snaps of horse hooves and metal greaves. She noted that morale was down, scanning the remaining forces, most of which had lost their leader. Fangbane wasted no time. He ordered them to continue marching, following Gaven's men. They had to join the main force to be in place with the rest of the fighters and annihilate the rebel force before reaching Ganmali.

Mirari's mind drifted to a day ten years ago when she was at home carrying a woven basket of toys that she shared with Salathiel and Gaven – unusual stones, bits of leftover string, crude wooden soldiers. On top were some fruits that she had snagged from the kitchen. She carried the basket into their room, hoping Salathiel and Gaven would spend time with her.

Salathiel was stretched out on the floor, his feet up against the wall as he immersed himself in a book. He was proficient enough to read at an elementary level, thanks to what she had taught him. Gaven was in a corner, sharpening the point of his wooden spear with a stone in hand.

As she entered, Gaven glanced at the basket of toys, and before she could say a word, he got up and walked out of the room. She felt the sting of his rejection.

"Where are you going?" she asked, but Gaven faded from her sight without responding.

"I think he's still a little shaken from yesterday," Salathiel explained without taking his eyes off the book.

Her body felt heavy, and her arms dropped. She was trying hard to forget what happened yesterday. What Salathiel claimed she had done might as well have been a lie – with no memory of the event, she could neither confirm nor deny his allegations – but she saw how Gaven looked at her differently and knew it was true.

"Doesn't he know I would never hurt him?" she said.

Salathiel tilted his head back and glanced at her. It was disturbingly quiet, and she was a perfect, motionless doll.

He set down the book. "That isn't the problem. What bothers him is he thinks you're lying. *And* you bested him. He's the fighter in this family. You destroyed the one thing he was proud of being better than the both of us in."

"But... I really don't remember anything, and I don't know how to use kore. Especially not fire, out of all things. You believe me, don't you?"

Salathiel's sweet smile was what she needed. She knew there was more to the story that he wouldn't say, but the fact was she had given Gaven a near-death experience... with powers she didn't know she had.

"Don't worry," Salathiel said. "He'll get over it."

But what if he never did? Even if Gaven had forgiven her for nearly hurting him, there was no doubt that since that day, he became a different person. Their pranks and jokes used to be good-natured. Now he was hostile, always challenging her and trying to be better than her. Gaven had liked her just fine as his playmate. But he couldn't live with himself knowing she could kick his ass six ways to Soli. That was what turned a boyish fantasy into an existential demand.

Mirari wondered if that's what drove him to leave home, to pursue the dangerous mission of training and becoming a fighter in Althaea. She let her pool of tears soak Joachim's shirt. He must've felt it.

"Don't blame yourself," he said. "You did your best."

"It wasn't enough," Mirari said. "Was I wrong to think I could stop him with mere words?"

"This is the nature of war, Miss Mirari."

"I know." But she didn't. Up until now, everything she learned about war was words on paper, her imagination. The feelings that came with it, all the adrenaline, blood, fear for life – she never expected the emotional toll. That was on top of the pain she was still carrying from losing Salathiel, and it was too much for her to handle.

"Does he really have to die, Joachim?" She croaked as she choked on tears. "Both of them? Is fate this cruel?"

She had never felt more useless. Her two closest friends were slipping from her reach, their promising lives ending abruptly in ways she believed she could've prevented. If that day had not happened – if she didn't let herself be consumed by an unknown power that hurt Gaven and tore his pride – would he have never joined the Althaea army and become this warlord that has taken so many lives? Would the three of them still be together?

"It's not over yet," Joachim said. "The main fight has yet to begin."

But Mirari knew that she had little chance of stopping Gaven now. She *had* a chance, it had been right in front of her, and she'd failed to make it work. In the face of five thousand soldiers, most of whom were desperate to claim his head, she was almost certain Gaven wouldn't make it out alive. This time she wouldn't be able to do anything about it.

"Mirari, Joachim," Fangbane called. She lifted her head off Joachim's back and stared at the masked man who was now riding parallel to them. "I've been informed that the rebel army at Ganmali has nearly tripled."

"What?" Joachim furrowed his brow. "So they outnumber us now?"

"I'm afraid so. They must've sent word for rebels to meet at Ganmali, and we underestimated their numbers."

"Sounds like you're not as good of a tactician as they say you are," Mirari said. "Maybe now you'll reconsider letting us fight."

"Hmm," Fangbane said and almost instantly replied. "No."

Mirari fumed. "Why can't you just admit you were wrong?"

"Because I wasn't. There are always unexpected consequences, especially in the chaos of battle. The art of a great battle plan is to set the stage to your best advantage; put yourself in the best position to take maximum advantage of your resources. That plan can be absolutely perfect on paper, but—"

"Okay, okay. So you're saying you're still perfect, that Commander Iffy and Region Leader Ahden's sacrifice was a part of your plan?"

"I'm not—"

"Admit it. Your *light brigade* strategy failed."

"It didn't fail," Fangbane sighed and shook his head. "We lowered their numbers and exhausted the rest, including the Valiant Tiger himself. As soon as a plan begins, you have to accept that something is absolutely guaranteed to go wrong. Maybe something catastrophic. You just don't know what that is – yet. The one thing that shouldn't happen is this: You should not be surprised. I'm telling you, Mirari, you should not be surprised that we lose people we didn't expect to lose."

Mirari understood what he was trying to say. "You're saying you're not guaranteeing Gaven's life anymore."

"I'm sorry, Mirari. I know you came all this way to save him, but we don't have much choice."

"You always have a choice," she said, eyes gleaming with determination. She wasn't ready to give up on Gaven just yet.

CHAPTER SIXTEEN

Valenian soldiers gathered at the peak of a rocky ridge, looking down on the boulder field as the sun reached the middle of the clear sky. Gaven and his army trotted down the slope with pitchforks, arrowheads tied to sticks, and even bows made of branches and thorns. The field was empty, but Gaven ordered the men into formation – defense from all sides with shielded calvaries in the middle.

"Looks like we have them now," Adder whispered to his fellow councilor as they laid low behind a mountain near the middle of the field.

Suzan waved her hand in the air, giving the signal to a troop a few yards down. He nodded and pulled a match from his pocket, carefully lighting the explosive in front of him before scampering away.

A rocket shot up into the sky and then burst in a shower of green sparks, bright enough to be seen for miles, even in daylight. Even Fangbane's army, on the other side of the ridge, noticed it.

"It's begun," Joachim said. But Mirari wasn't exactly sure what that meant. Did the beginning of this battle mark the end of the revolution? Or was the flare the bell for Gaven to hang?

When Gaven saw the rocket explode above, he felt a jolt of adrenaline spike through his brain. It was a signal flare – but for whom?

Then one of his scouts called to him. "My Lord! Look!"

Gaven turned, and before the scout could say another word, Gaven saw the wave of grey-painted banners and heavily armored foot soldiers charging down from the left side of the ridge.

At first, he thought it might be the same brigade of raiders that was sent out to harass his column. But the mass of troops moving from behind the rocky mountain grew larger and larger. He could see banners and blocks of troops in various uniforms, mostly those from Valenian territories. The sight was strange to him – to see Valenian soldiers on Althaean soil. It confirmed that the Council had sent people from across the land to put an end to their march.

Any chance to withdraw was over with. Fine. Nowhere to go but forward. He did a quick calculation as the last of those soldiers popped out from behind the mountain. Two, three hundred?

He unsheathed his spear and pointed it to the mountain. "Charge!"

Instantly, the men on the left began to run toward the enemy, sticks in the air, their cries mightier than the winds across Lake Urabe.

A young rebel faced the oncoming battle line of spear carriers, rolling at the front like a bristling wave. "This is my goddamn empire, you swine, sprout-munching farters!" He led a savage, if not suicidal, counter-charge into the heart of Valenia's ocean of spearmen.

Gaven was ready to join until he heard the wisp of a flying projectile.

He swung his gaze away from the troops just in time to see a second rocket soar into the vast, clear sky. The explosion of sapphire sparks glowed nicely against the pale blue above. Without hesitating, accepting the clear change in the situation, he called to the men on the far right.

"Onward, with me!" He snapped his horse into a forward charge, and the rest of his units who had not yet engaged in battle sprinted down the hill with him. Whoever that signal was for, he couldn't risk wasting time getting to the armory.

There was an objective before him. Gaven's confidence vacillated, and he was forced to replace it with the iron will of military discipline. A feeling of grim determination filled him now.

The farther down the mountain he got, the better he could see the streak of cavalry units seeping toward them like a wave of spilled oil. Their dark cloaks enveloped the field, covering the land from mountain to mountain.

Nearly a thousand were following their leaders at the front, all of whom were familiar. Next to a big brawler was a man Gaven knew was dying to claim his head. His long hair wavered with his cloak as his horse sprinted straight for Gaven. He had a happy grin and an immense thirst for blood, Gaven's blood specifically.

The dark soldiers spread into an enveloping umbrella from the north and west, slamming shut the trap which surrounded the band of revolutionaries.

"Show me what you got, Kitten!" Shiba yelled as he took a swing at Gaven.

Gaven ducked, then quickly realized that the slash was not for him but his horse. His horse stumbled to the ground, a fountain of blood coming out from its neck. Shiba leapt off his horse with a dagger in each hand. Gaven rolled out of the way just in time. He picked up the nearest boulder and threw it at Shiba. It went right through him as he disappeared into a mist.

Gaven felt something reach from behind and yank his shoulders back. His arms were locked by a big brawler whose arms were twice as thick as his. He felt his feet lift off the ground. They both arched backward and fell hard to the ground.

"Why don't you surrender and make this easier for us?" Neo offered, but Gaven gave a hardened grunt and kicked him in his treasures. He broke free from Neo but was quickly confined again by a substance rising from the ground – Shiba's shadow. Legs trapped and gradually losing control, Gaven didn't have time to prepare for the hard punch to his face.

"Die, Althaean scum!" Shiba roared as he pulled his hand back for another punch.

But Gaven had faced Shiba before. He had learned his ways and how he used his trump card. It was no longer a threat to him. His shadow was like rubber, stretchy and sturdy enough to hold down a brawler, but at best, that was all it could do. Shiba's shadow was all for show, a distraction to make enemies turn away from him. At the right angle, Gaven knew he could break.

He squeezed his hands, twisted and ripped the shadow apart like paper. He rammed his head right into Shiba's chest and raised his own fist, charging it with the energy raging in his body. He pulsed forward. Neo lunged in front of Shiba and caught it, barely, the force making him slide back a few inches. The men were now locked in fists.

"What's gotten into you?" Neo asked again.

"Do not stop me, brawler!" Gaven roared as he pushed harder into Neo.

Shiba was ready to kick back in but stopped as he was nearly run over by a cavalry soldier, who readied his sword in the hope that if Shiba wasn't trampled, he would meet his fate at the end of the soldier's blade. Shiba dodged both, sneering at the peasant who dared to interfere. Two more riders joined the soldier. They were better equipped than the majority of peasants, carrying silver spears and slip-on breastplates taken from fallen soldiers from the enemy's side.

"I'll take on this scum, Your Honor," Eoin cried to Gaven as his horse neighed, rose on its hind legs, and charged at Neo.

Shiba now had a clear view of Gaven. He snickered as he cracked his knuckles. "How 'bout it? You, me, one-on-one. For old times' sake."

Gaven narrowed his eyes. He twirled his spear above his head, then positioned himself in a lunge, blade pointing forward as he waited for his opponent's first move.

A scout from the Royal Army weaved through Shiba's engaged forces and up the side of the mountain to where the councilors overlooked the fight. He pulled over to Councilor Adder and whispered a message in his ear.

"What?" he hissed.

"What's wrong?" Suzan asked.

"There's roughly three thousand rebels on the other side of Ganmali, and they're infiltrating the armory as we speak. The division we've stationed there is being overwhelmed."

"Three thousand?" They had only planted one thousand at the armory. "Where did they all come from? The rebels couldn't possibly have planned this."

"Perhaps not," Adder agreed. "Maybe it's a coincidence that both forces arrived at the same time. But we need to stop them before they find the weapons."

Adder gestured the scout off his horse and replaced him in the saddle.

"What do you think you're doing?" Suzan demanded.

"Sending back up. If they get their hands on the armory, we'll be lost." He grasped the reins, then pointed to the cavalry near the bottom of the ridge, jousting with horseless peasants and winning. "I'm taking Shiba and Neo with me. Five hundred should do."

"But they're already in position. And what about Gaven?"

Adder turned his horse toward the downward path to Ganmali. "Fangbane's unit should be here any moment. You two can handle him, can't you?"

He snapped the reins and galloped down the hill. He pulled up to Shiba, who was well engaged with his sworn enemy. Adder slid his horse between them with elegant skill, precision, and little care of the dangers of being in between two fighters.

"Shadow Soldier, Silver Fist," he called. "Find a horse, now. We're going to the armory."

"What?" Shiba sneered. "You want me to dishonor the duel?"

"Dishonor the Council or dishonor your pride. You choose." Adder shifted his eyes to Gaven, who did nothing. "Will this be a problem, Valiant Tiger?"

Gaven seemed to have respected their change in strategy and was willing to let them go without any resistance. Adder narrowed his eyes, taking note of Gaven's zombie-like demeanor. His face was bland and more oblivious than a ringed gopher in the face of a saberlion. They stared at each other but said nothing.

Adder snapped his horse into a sprint down the hill, rallying along as many rogue cavalry units as he could along the way.

"C'mon," Neo nudged Shiba, who had the reins of both their horses in his hands. Shiba sneered and glared at Gaven.

"Don't die until I get back," Shiba spat as he got on his horse. "I want to be the one to take your head."

Gaven simply stared. He saw the departing troops, believing the fight had now returned to his favor. Though he didn't know of their progress, he knew the rebels on the other side of Ganmali were proving to be the distraction he needed to win this battle.

He rallied Eoin and the rest of his men to continue fighting off the rest of these invaders.

CHAPTER SEVENTEEN

F angbane's units arrived at the ridge, but instead of diving straight from the top of the hill, they eased around the edge to where Suzan's command was stationed. As soon as she saw Fangbane and the hundreds of troops following him, she breathed a sigh of relief.

"What took you so long?" she said. "Adder went off with Shiba's team to defend the armory. We need your squad in there as soon as possible."

Fangbane looked down at the boulder field, thousands of men engaged in a chaotic battle. It was a slaughter of such ferocity that several of the peasants found themselves puking on the bloodied ground. Fangbane's reaction was unknowable, concealed behind the silvery shine of his finely polished helmet mask, but Starlight looked like she was about to puke herself.

"How many?" she asked. "Here, and the force at the armory?"

"Nearly five thousand in total."

Fangbane did quick mental math, then shook his head. He wasn't worried about the armory – Adder, Shiba, and Neo would be a nightmare to anyone who crossed their paths. But without them on the frontline, they could no longer win the main battle by a landslide. He predicted it would be close, down to the last hundred men.

Fangbane sighed. "I'm sorry, I didn't expect so many rebels. Suzan, I'm not sure if we can win this."

"What do you mean?" She noticed that his group was missing a few people. "Where's Ahden? And Erel?"

That was his other problem. He had lost two valuable fighters during the night raid. While they did eliminate a good fraction of Gaven's forces and injured Gaven himself, the two were not here to fight the battle they were desperately needed to fight.

"I'm here, Your Grace," Erel called, shoving her way to the front. She was patched with bandages over her arm and torso, a brutal sight for a slash-and-run operation. "But I'm afraid Region Leader Ahden and Commander Iphigenia did not make it."

Suzan was at a loss for words. "You look bad."

"But I will keep fighting," Erel promised. "We all will."

Behind her, a mix of young Althaean men, Iphigenia's Valkyries, and celtas from Valenia stood tall – they were ready to fight to the death.

Mirari was uneasy about the massacre unfolding in front of her. She had only one thing occupying her mind – where was Gaven?

It seemed that the men down there were out to butcher anything that moved. She knew they no longer had any intention to capture Gaven alive.

"Go forward," Fangbane called to Erel and the rest of the units in her command. Without hesitation, they charged down the hill, joining the rest of their allies.

"You're worried this won't be enough," Suzan said, reading Fangbane's mannerisms.

"It's possible, but…" Fangbane shook his head. "We'll be

cutting it too close. To see this many die? For what purpose? I was hoping they would surrender before we had to slaughter all of them, but this… I don't understand. Why do they still fight?"

ON THE OTHER SIDE, Gaven and his men watched as another force rolled down the hill from the right. Erel's army, the small brigade that had attacked him earlier, was finally joining the battle. He watched the wall of fighting men roll like a wave.

One of his soldiers cursed, "Bloody claws, they're shucking us like corn!" He turned and screamed to his company of Nanakan miners and fishermen. "Let's pile these corpses!"

Eoin looked up at the scrambling wave of soldiers, then faced his leader. "You want me to take care of that, sir?" he asked.

"Please."

Eoin charged ahead, shouting, "These are the jaws of Inferna, brothers. Let's get in there and bust out some teeth!" With several hundred wild, desperate men behind him, Eoin charged at the oncoming blitz.

Fangbane and Suzan watched from their vantage point. She shook her head.

"Will I have to roll up my sleeves here?" she sighed.

"It's likely," Fangbane said. "It's too bad your successor didn't work out."

"It is, indeed, too bad."

Something tugged in Fangbane's mind. Thoughts. Ideas. Things that would interrupt his already fragile plan. He turned to Mirari. She had her hand on her lips, presumably going over strategies to save Gaven.

"You," he warned, "will not fight."

"Again?" Mirari snapped. "Aren't you short-handed?"

"You're not trained for the frontline. You run into the fight, and you will disrupt our strategy. These commanders know where their men are at all times. You disrupt their flow, you not only risk your own life but theirs."

"I obeyed your orders last time," Mirari reminded him. "And now Ahden and Iffy are gone. Thousands more may die." She paused. "Are dying. So no, I don't believe you have this under control. I don't believe you have any intention of saving Gaven."

"Let the fighters handle this battle. You have no idea—"

But Mirari was not listening. She was drawn to the image of Gaven as she spotted him moving among dozens of bodies, leaping, slashing, and ripping like a beast.

"There he is!" she yelled to Joachim, ignoring every word from Fangbane's mouth.

Joachim tugged her arm. "Mirari, listen to reason—"

"No! There may be nothing I can do for Sal, but Gaven is still alive, right here. I can't turn my back again. I won't let him die. I have to try."

But she realized she need not speak further. There was a sudden change in his countenance. His whip hung loosely by his side as his fingers traced the intricate weave of the leather. She could see how he changed his stance; he looked less like the dancer he was when she was in training and more aggressive like a panther.

"I know," Joachim said. His heavy sigh told her he still didn't agree with her decision but was ready to stand by whatever she did, no matter how ridiculous.

Her face bloomed into a light smile. "This is the last task I ask of you, Joachim. Fight with me. After this, you will be a free man. That is my will."

He lowered his head in an elegant bow. "It would be my honor, Milady."

She turned, moving down the battlement toward Gaven.

"Blood-sucking toe ticklers!" Fangbane shouted. "Damn that hellion to the deepest dungeons on Sufferer's Island. They're going to get killed."

"You should've never brought them along, Fang," Suzan said.

"Well?" Starlight tilted her head, glancing between her husband and the runaways. "You're not going to stop her?"

Fangbane watched Mirari leap down from the rocky side of the mountain, avoiding every soldier in battle and ignoring the dangers of the steep cliff. She hit the ground running, with Joachim close behind.

"I... don't think I will."

Starlight whispered, "But, dear—""

"Sorren may have been wrong," he said, as much as the words stung him. "I think we should take the gamble."

Starlight shook her head. She couldn't imagine what good could come from letting an untrained maiden face off the rabid warrior. Still, she had faith in Fangbane's decisions. She prayed for their safety and rallied her healers toward the injured.

For a moment, Mirari and Joachim stood in awe, watching as Gaven felled man after man. It seemed the more he killed, the more soldiers crowded around him, forming a wide ring. If they all rushed him, it would be over. Only nobody dared to go first. He was dripping with buckets of gore like he bathed in the stuff.

"Come on! Who's next!" he screamed at the gathering ring of enemy soldiers. Beyond this knot of combatants, the sounds of battle were slowing down.

"Well? Are there none but cowards here?" Gaven said, his lips curled in savage rage. He scanned the surrounding faces. Many eyes dropped to the ground. He tried to find a single look to challenge him.

There wasn't an ounce of resignation in him. In fact, he wasn't the least bit concerned by the enemies surrounding him. He held his spear up for them to see, circling them, so they all got a good look. It was layered with blood, some dried and black, some fresh and dripping. A single jewel of dripping blood formed at the tip; he watched how the sun winked at the droplet just before it fell to the earth.

"We will," Mirari said, turning to Joachim. "We will be the ones to fight him."

"Mirari." Joachim raised a hand and dropped it in a slow downward motion, a reminder to focus on her breath before jumping in battle. She did as he instructed, exhaling. "You should know if he's truly possessed, there's a possibility that the real Gaven may not return."

She looked down at the hilt of her sword – a weapon that would soon be bathed in its first blood. The thought had crossed her mind before, but she didn't want to face it.

Joachim looked at her sternly. "If it comes to you or him, I will have no other choice."

Mirari swallowed. Her body suddenly felt too heavy to hold, but she nodded and drew her sword. At the sound of metal, Gaven turned to her. He let out a light chuckle.

"A duo, huh?" Gaven said. "Fine. For the old man and his lady, I'll honor it." He spun his spear overhead, then crouched with the weapon pointed at them.

Joachim flicked his arm lightning quick, his whip lashing out and catching Gaven across his cheek. He didn't flinch from the hit, but his eyes burned with rage as blood seeped from the welt.

"You have my mark," Joachim said. "Your defeat is at hand."

Gaven roared, swinging his spear overhead, aiming for Joachim's head only to be met with a clash of steel as Mirari blocked the fatal blow. Joachim circled around her left. He launched two throwing stars at Gaven. Gaven swept up dirt with enough force to deflect the stars, then drove through the falling dirt with a stab. Mirari countered with a chop that drove the spear point downward, and Joachim lunged with his two daggers, cutting two neat red grooves in Gaven's forearm and shoulder before spinning away.

Stone spikes rose from the ground to pierce Joachim.

Mirari gasped as she and Joachim were separated by the spikes. Gaven spun toward her.

"Little girls shouldn't play with swords." Gaven leered and charged. Her training kept her outside of his range as she deflected the spear with her blade.

His reach was too great. She had to find a way inside his defense.

But what would she do when she got in there? She couldn't stab him... could she?

He swung his spear, leaving his body wide and exposed. Taking the advantage, she slipped inside his spear range and swung hard for his right arm, hoping to maim him. But Gaven was too quick and brought the stave of his spear around to catch her swing. The impact jarred her arm, and she pushed against their crossed weapons, her eyes wide with pain. She didn't expect him to be so strong.

Gaven's breath was hot and rancid. He was so close she could smell his sweat as he locked eyes with her. Her heart leaped in her chest. The person before her wasn't Gaven. It was only a desperate, hungry beast.

Gaven stumbled as Joachim's whip found its way around his neck. He growled as Joachim yanked him backward and slammed him into the stone spikes.

Joachim came around the other side of the spikes, the whip around his shoulders as he sent a storm of throwing stars at Gaven. Gaven growled, raising an arm, deflecting the blades with his forearm, and blocking Mirari's sword with the spear in his other hand.

Joachim kept away this time, throwing star after star. Mirari followed her retainer, stepping into a rhythm of attack and retreat. Every time she stepped away, a hail of stars fell upon Gaven. They kept up the attack even after Joachim's stars were depleted. He was on his last six daggers. Joachim lashed at Gaven to cover Mirari for what he hoped would be one final blow.

Mirari dashed in, now enraged. She couldn't explain it, but

in that moment, she knew that this creature was no longer her childhood friend. It was something pure evil.

Power rushed into her limbs; she attacked Gaven with a fury she had never known.

But he was simply playing with her, letting her efforts tickle his thirst for an entertaining show. He grabbed the whip confining his wrist and pulled it forward. Joachim was forced to loosen his grip just enough.

Mirari missed her swipe, and he reached straight for the hilt of her sword, holding it down with the force of a tiger. His knee came up, right into her stomach. Mirari doubled forward. With a head of titanium, he slammed into her.

Agonizing pain engulfed her, but she was too overwhelmed to cry out.

The beast was ready to play some more, but before he could force her up, he felt a strong lash against his back, shattering his cracked armor and engraving a fresh gash. He turned just in time to deflect a dagger aimed for his heart. Joachim quickly lunged forward and collided into him head first like a seasoned battle bull. That was Joachim's style – serving a taste of his opponent's own medicine.

Gaven staggered. This level of skilled resistance was a shock to him. He smiled, reveling in his first real challenge of the campaign. "My apology, old man. You do stand as a champion among these vile worms. I'm truly impressed."

Joachim felt warmth flowing down his chest now. He glanced at his white linen shirt, a foot-long slice cut through the cloth where a long, shallow wound lay across his chest, just like the one he inflicted on Gaven's back. Joachim flashed his eyes back to Gaven – afraid he had looked away too long, even in that split second. But Gaven wasn't in any hurry. His eyes seemed to be on fire, excited to have blood flowing.

"I will be sorry to see an end to you, sir," Gaven said. "Now, show me everything you have."

The sting of Gaven's blade against his left shoulder ignited Joachim, and he began to attack with all he had.

Gaven heard the maiden's battle cry. Mirari charged forward with her sword in both hands held up high, ready to strike like a blacksmith striking an anvil. She was enraged, losing all sense of logic and tactic.

A simple side step was all he needed to do to avoid her charge. Her sharp blade slipped into a stone spike, lodged and stuck in the rock.

"Feces of the fae!" Mirari cursed, trying to tug her sword out. Joachim jumped in, ready to cover for her.

But Mirari saw a faint smile on the tiger's lips.

"Joachim, no!" she cried, but it was too late.

A spout of earth beneath Joachim's feet sent him high into the air. With his kore, Joachim's hands guided the earth under his control. The rocks that had lifted him off the ground now molded into pellets and fired themselves at the Valiant Tiger.

Mirari gave one final cry and yanked her sword out from the rock, charging at Gaven while his vision was still blocked as he shielded his face from the pellets. She hacked at him, but he didn't need to see her to block her swing. Then with a turn of his wrist, his blade jabbed forward.

It missed Mirari by a hair... and lodged into the fighter behind her.

Mirari turned, face drained white as she saw her retainer skewered from front to back. Joachim acted as if it was nothing. He pressed forward, twisting and pulling the shaft out of his chest, tossing it to the side and pulling Gaven into a hug with a dagger in hand.

Gaven sneered, his hand on the blade lodged in his shoulder, and staggered away from him.

"Ah, good," Joachim choked while his knees trembled, gradually losing strength. "I was starting to wonder if you know how to bleed."

Mirari caught him as he stumbled to his knees. Tears blurred her eyes. "No, Joachim, no, you can't die. Get up!"

"I am sorry, dear one, I cannot." He held a hand to her face, his eyes drifting off as death approached him. "You have a strength within you, child, that you could not imagine. Go forward with all your might... never... settle for less." He tried to say more, but his time had come. Mirari held on to the one person who had always put her first.

"I have done my part," Joachim wheezed. "Now finish him."

"I... can't do it. Not without you."

"I know you can." He embraced her one last time. "Be that fearless girl I raised... Miss Hale."

"Joachim!" she screamed, her voice crackling like glass. "Get up!" And when he didn't respond, she screamed again. "I command you to!"

The man had never defied an order from his lady until now.

Before Gaven could take the life of the grieving maiden, another whip struck him. It fastened around his leg, and he fell face-first into the ground.

"That's enough," Suzan hissed. "This duel is over. Now you fight the rest of us."

Her entrance was a delight – a new challenger. But before he could take her on, he was ambushed by the fighters who once stood on the sideline.

Mirari wailed with no restraint, but she wasn't the only one. She saw more fighters launch onto Gaven, desperate to take his head. Joachim's death enraged them and gave the army hope to take down the last of the rebellion. They aimed for Gaven's head, unheeding the Council's orders. They were thirsty to earn the title of the fighter who slew the Valiant Tiger, the one who ended the rebellion.

Fangbane sprinted to Mirari's side, dragging her away from Joachim. Starlight joined her husband. She gasped as her gaze fell upon Joachim.

"Oh dear," Starlight whispered and looked at her husband, who was also left speechless. Joachim was punctured front to back, innards exposed. Even with the best healers in the empire, the chances of his survival were minimal. If he did survive, an infection would follow. In cases like these, healers would be advised to let the fighter die with honor, but Starlight wasn't ready to give up, especially not for this grieving girl. She placed her head over Joachim's heart. "He still has a pulse."

She waved over two medics who arrived with a stretcher. They brought Joachim down the hill toward their established medical tents.

Turning back to Mirari and her desperate cries, Starlight took her and pulled her in for a hug. Her shoulder absorbed Mirari's tears as she stroked her head. She gave her husband a look, and he returned a nod.

A soft blue glow illuminated from her hand. She kept it on Mirari's head until she slumped over in slumber, tears falling as the last of her strength drifted away.

"She has seen enough," Starlight said, lifting Mirari onto her back. "I'll take her to the tent."

The law of the large had worked its inescapable will – the rebels were beaten. There were pockets of fighting still raging, but the outcome was not in doubt.

Even though his rebels were crushed or had scattered and his insurrection had failed, Gaven still wanted a fight to the death. He was isolated and alone, facing an entire army. His continued resistance was hopeless. He didn't stand a chance.

But Gaven fought with no mercy.

Starlight took a few steps forward, then stopped abruptly. She looked over her shoulder and waited.

"That's not possible…" she muttered.

Fangbane furrowed his brow, sensing the panic in his wife. Her relaxer should've kept Mirari knocked out for at least half an hour. He brought his attention back to Mirari. They waited to see if she would wake up or if she was treading in light sleep.

Mirari's eyes fluttered open.

What concerned Fangbane more was what he couldn't sense. A conscious body stared back at him, but he heard nothing. The slant in her brows implied that she wasn't pleased. He noticed a glow in her eyes, reflecting more than tears. Was it a trick of the sun, or was it something profoundly dangerous? Whatever it was, none of it was calculated.

CHAPTER EIGHTEEN

M irari burst with energy, flailing and kicking Starlight with such force that she lost her balance. They both tumbled to the ground.

Mirari shuffled to her feet, but Fangbane locked her in his arms before she could run off. She was desperate to run to Gaven, who had retrieved his spear and was hacking away at the remaining brave soldiers.

"Mirari, stop!" Fangbane said.

"Do not touch me!" she roared, stretching her elbows in an attempt to pull his arms apart. Fangbane wasn't going to let her go, but a small ball of red flames in her left hand distracted him. Fangbane froze.

He had no idea she knew how to wield fire. Why hadn't she used it earlier? And what was she planning to do with it?

He tried focusing on her mind again, his forehead creasing behind his mask as he searched for a mental opening. But his mind went through her as if her body didn't exist. There was nothing.

She hurled it at him in an upward jab to his face. There was a loud *clang!* when her fist hit his mask. He stumbled backward, slightly dazed.

Mirari hurled a fireball at his feet. It missed, creating a patch of flames in the grass between him and her.

"Saint Lorus' firecrackers!" Fangbane cursed as he tried to regain his focus. He wasn't sure he could restrain her again. Stopping a grieving girl was not the same as stopping an enraged warrior with fire abilities.

They heard the gallop of horses approaching from the lower field as they made their way up the hill led by the Shadow Soldier and the Silver Fist.

Perfect timing. Fangbane sighed with relief. That meant the armory was secured and under control. He knew he could leave that in Councilor Adder's hands and focus on the battle before them.

Out of my way.

He finally heard Mirari's voice. But it was different. It didn't sound like her thoughts, more like she was sending him a telepathic message.

Fangbane was disoriented, hesitant, and uncertain, but he felt obligated to yield to her command.

But, like a single thread that could unravel the finest stitches, he recognized that he was looking at the event that would change everything.

Almost as if he had been trapped by her flames, he could only stand and watch her approach Gaven. The troops parted for Mirari as they murmured and gasped in disbelief. A cacophony of surprise, curiosity, and confusion passed through the crowd. The battle-hardened soldiers gaped at this wisp of a thing.

Gaven burst into laughter upon seeing Mirari again.

"You lost your duel, maiden. Don't try your luck twice." He turned to the rest of the crowd. His laughter faded, seeing that no one else was willing to approach him. "What is this? You miserable cowards send a maiden to do—"

He never finished. Her bloodcurdling scream struck like a wave of force as she charged at him with astonishing speed, sword in hand. He barely got his spear up in time to block her first attack. The crowd watched in spellbound silence.

She slashed and parried, not giving Gaven a second of rest. Gaven had to check his distance to close with her, to cut her in half with his own weapon. Not long after he slashed at her, she tossed her sword away as if it were just a bother. Mirari brought her hands together. The flames she created were almost hypnotic. She shrieked an unearthly, bloodcurdling roar as she charged straight for Gaven.

Gaven seemed to have grown cautious now, barely dodging her fiery attack, darting left and right. He blocked her hand with the spear, handling it with a mastery no warrior could match.

"You're getting a little wild there," he said. "A real warrior doesn't give in to revenge."

A transparent barrier shimmered into existence, forming a clear arch. It enclosed the two fighters, sealing them off in an invisible but impenetrable dome.

MIRARI mulled over the source of the force field, forgetting that there were others on the battlefield who wanted to intervene. It was sturdy — an impressive display of kore mastery — and she could use it in her favor.

Almost as if those outside knew of her plan, a dark shadow filled the ground underneath Gaven. He didn't seem to notice the shadowmancer's ability until it rose and seized his ankles with human-shaped hands. Gaven lost his balance in the struggle and fell to the ground.

Mirari spread her arms wide, flames in each hand. They were larger than anything she had hurled yet, but she let the flames flare even more. They poured along the side of the barricade, giving her full command.

She was caressed in her wave of flames. A relaxing feeling of freedom settled over her, but she was displeased seeing her foe. Was she awakened as a gesture of kindness or to be executed? Her instincts leaned toward the latter.

This fighter before her, ambitious as he was stupid, was supposed to be the best among the mortals. The scrapes he inflicted proved it. Or maybe it showed that Mirari's power was yet to fully awaken.

Mirari gathered the aura in her hands again, its warmth bathing her skin in the soothing way she had missed. They were hers, the red flames of fate.

Mirari hurtled them, choosing speed at the cost of accuracy. The flame whizzed past her target, just two feet off, but the fighter was prepared for it and managed to take a swing at the very thing meant to destroy him. The fireballs bounced, skipped off the dirt, and came back toward her. Mirari didn't bother to dodge it. She let the fire return to her body.

"Have you not done enough damage?" she hissed.

The heat inside the dome was searing. It was worse than a sauna now, and sweat drenched the two fighters. Gaven knew there was nothing he could do to free himself, and he could only hope to deflect the next barrage of fire.

"Who are you?" Gaven challenged, spear pointed up and ready to swing at her again. But Mirari could sense from the quiver in his voice that only a fraction of his courage remained. The flames had spooked him as they should have. There was no chance he was getting out of this dome alive.

"Send your master my regards." Mirari raised her hand, ready to claim the man's soul. But a tug in her mind held her back. Her muscles refused to move, stiff as hardened clay.

Don't hurt him...

"Tch," she hissed, frustrated at the lack of control over her body. "You can't be serious..."

She only took her eyes off Gaven for a second, and his spear came at her. Mirari grabbed it with both her hands, stopping it inches from her head. Gaven twisted his wrist, and his spear came down on her shoulder. A gash split open where it met her skin.

"Blood-sucking demons," she cursed and hurled a fireball at Gaven. He dodged it and struck the barrier again behind her, causing it to erupt in a shower of tiny sparks.

Gaven lunged at her, but she grabbed his throat, his spear now in her hand.

"Tell me," she seethed with a thrill coursing through her veins. "Do you want to die by your own blade or in her hands?"

He clawed at her, wheezing for a breath.

Her greatest weapon was not a blade, nor was it her throne of flames. She tossed the spear and looked deep into Gaven's soul, focusing on the impurities rooted in his mind. They were drawn to her touch, trawled from their host like an ocean current. Unable to resist her pull, the dark mist resurfaced around Gaven's body. One glare was all it took for the mist to be seared by the flames around it. Gone without a trace. Few would know of its existence, and that was the way it should've been.

As Gaven's mind was purified, his struggle for air became human again.

But even though he was released from the curse now, she wasn't going to let him live. These men who fell victim to their own guilt would only be taken advantage of again.

To her surprise, he didn't struggle. This warrior, who knew no quit, didn't fight for his life. He breathed as though he accepted defeat, eyes full of shame, and all he could think about was thanking her for saving him.

He whispered something as he stared into her eyes. It was only a slither, not loud enough for her to make out... but his voice had a strange effect on her body, and she felt her arm grow heavy.

Her? Pity? Nonsense. No, those were not her feelings. Her host was regaining control.

She felt her hand shake, her mind fading. She let go, dropping Gaven's frail body on the small part of the ground that wasn't consumed in fire. He fell, lifeless. Perhaps even dead?

Control was slipping from her once again. The tug in her chest, a voice in her head... it was her.

'Roselyn' was fighting back.

Her flames were fueled, pounding against the surrounding force field, pressing harder, growing hotter — with her desperate efforts to regain control — until it shattered.

A wave of air rushed into her lungs as clouds of smoke and ash blanketed the boulder field. She could hear the people around them in a panic as they began to sputter and choke on the fumes.

She couldn't call it a victory. The true enemy was still out there, and control was far from her reach. Even if her strength returned, what more could she gain from this battle?

She sunk to her knees. She couldn't feel her fingers anymore. Her mind went numb, and the flames returned within her, back inside in a deep slumber.

But she knew it would only be a matter of time until she was summoned again. The real war was about to begin.

The Story Continues in the Alliance Trilogy

Book 1: Knights of the Alliance
Available Now

Book 2: Birth of Resilience
Coming Summer 2023

Book 3: Edge of Divergence
Coming Summer 2024

BONUS SCENE AHEAD!

FIRE

Roselyn forced open her heavy eyelids.

She found herself staring at the back of Salathiel's head. His arms locked around her legs as he carried her over his shoulder. They were still in the forest – she recognized the white, scrawny trunks rising above piles of crisp brown and orange leaves that had long fallen from their branches. They were almost home.

"You awake?" Salathiel asked, feeling her body shift on his back.

"Mhm," she mumbled. "Did I fall asleep?"

Salathiel bit his lip and thought, I knocked your skull against a tree to keep you from incinerating me in a fit of madness. Instead, only one word came out of his mouth. "Yeah."

Roselyn lifted her head to look for Gaven. He trudged alongside Salathiel, carrying the boar they caught. She was impressed, but not surprised. The boar must've been half of his body weight, but Gaven didn't appear to be struggling in the slightest. He was strong, seemingly getting stronger with each hunt. Soon, she and Salathiel would just be getting in his way.

Gaven shifted his eyes on her. They were cold as ice, threatening and unwelcoming.

She could tell he was holding back anger. Step after step on the dirt ground, they kept walking and he just kept glaring at her.

"Who pissed in your soup today?" she asked.

Instantly confrontational, Gaven shouted, "You!"

"Me? What did I do?"

Salathiel groaned. He didn't intend on having this discussion. If Roselyn kept a secret from them, there was a reason, and he was willing to wait until she was ready to explain herself.

Gaven didn't feel the same. The two children began hissing at each other with their piercing voices.

Gaven yelled, "You're such a liar!"

"What did I lie about?"

"You said you couldn't use kore!"

"I can't! Why would I lie about that?"

"So you can roast Sal and I when we're caught off guard! Get rid of us so you can have a family to yourself! That's what all you nobles are like. You have to take everything—"

"Gav!" Salathiel hushed, but their voices continue to echo over him.

"What are you on about?" Roselyn asked. She leaned toward Gaven, arm stretched out as if she was ready to yank his ear off. But Salathiel stepped back, making sure the two kept their distance.

"Are you really going to play dumb?" Gaven asked through gritting teeth. "We both saw it. You know how to use kore."

"This is ridiculous." She turned away. "Sal? Say something."

But before Salathiel could answer, Gaven said, "You nearly started a forest fire!"

"What do you mean? When?"

"Just now. Before you decided to take a nap." Gaven pointed out, sarcastically.

"You're lying. He's lying, right Sal?"

Salathiel had a chance to speak, but he didn't take it. Where would he start? What could he say without sounding like he was taking a side?

"Gav, let it go," he said.

"What? You're really going to let her get away with it?"

"She went through a lot. Let her rest."

Roselyn stuck her tongue out at him. "You're bad at lying."

"He's not lying, Roselyn," Salathiel continued. "We saw you control flames with your hands, and since we live in a forest, you can't use that power around here again. Understand?"

Roselyn tilted her head. "What are you two going on about? I can't use kore. Look."

Roselyn raised her hands to the air, stretched them high and flailed. Nothing happened.

"It's alright if you don't want to talk about it," Salathiel sighed. "But Roselyn, you really shouldn't be keeping things from us."

"I'm telling you," Roselyn said, pouting, her cheeks puffed and brows furrowed. "If I could use kore, I'd be showing it off, not hiding it. And out of all elements, fire? Do you know how hard it is for someone to control fire? It would be impossible for someone with no kore to be able to—"

Roselyn froze. This conversation was beginning to sound all too familiar.

If the boys were telling the truth, it would be like the time they found her in the woods – she would have no injuries. She looked down at her disheveled clothes and exposed skin. She was unhurt, barring some dirt spots on her left sleeve. On closer inspection, she found it wasn't dirt, but a soft ash.

She peeked at Gaven. Though his face was smeared with soot, mostly on his neck and a little on his cheek, he appeared fine. Roselyn leered at Salathiel's face and noticed a fresh scratch that was now healed.

"What is that?" Roselyn asked, running her finger over the scar.

"I hurt myself," Salathiel explained. "It's nothing."

"With... what?" Roselyn grew more concerned. "Did... I hurt you?"

"No—"

"But you nearly killed me," Gaven interrupted. Yes, Roselyn was used to his tantrums, but this was different. His eyes only spoke hate. He looked at her like a stranger, someone he didn't trust.

And she understood; she wasn't sure if she could trust herself either. If she was the fire – and she was immune to her own flames – then she could kill.

Guilt sluiced through her body – then a cold rush of fear and anxiety. Roselyn wasn't sure how to offer him comfort. She was being accused of something she couldn't remember.

"I- I'm sorry, Gav. But really, I don't remember anything."

Gaven scoffed, turning away. "I don't buy that."

This was even more frightening – her lack of control when it happened. There had been no warning sign. She felt like a ticking time bomb, a threat to anyone too close to her.

She was lucky that no one got hurt this time. There was no guarantee it would be the same if it were to happen again.

APPENDIX

FIGHTER CLASS – Fighters are trained in one of four styles:
Aegis – bow users in touch with nature and animals.
Celta – healers & spellcasters who are masters of kore.
Paragon – brawlers & warriors with close-combat weaponry.
Umbra – mixed-weapon fighters with self-defense techniques.

HALE INVENTIONS – The Hale family discovered they could process raw crystals containing energy, known as hāstals, and enhanced them with kore to create new technology.
Aulāce – indestructible shackles made with kore and alloys.
Aulōg – a lock coded with one's aura. Used to secure doors.
Clōve – a hāstal-sewn glove capable of communication.
Comstōne – quartz geodes that direct sounds to other stones.
Kinastōne – a barrel-shaped geode used to generate energy.
Kirinvā Stone – a hāstal rumored to offer protection.
Kōnvoy – a caravan that transports large shipping materials.
Lumastōne – a glowing pebble that replaces candlelight.
Oriōn – a cube that crafts a geometric replica of landscapes.
Renastōne – palm-sized stones that amplify healing abilities.
Visōr – a platform that mirrors images.

TERMINOLOGY – These jargons and commercial goods are unique to the land of the three empires.

Aster Spells – an advanced category of spells.

Aura – the spiritual energy unique to each individual.

Bitterworm – an invertebrate good for harvesting vegetables.

Buzzbean – a mixture of nuts and herbs used as tea.

Cepha Metal – a dense material that blocks psychic energy.

Cryphedeon – a disc-shaped herbal flower used for flavoring.

Featherpit – someone who wears feathers for fashion, directed at insulting Minettan culture.

Flatty/Flat-Faced – a derogatory word comparing two-faced Althaeans with the sides of a flat coin.

Galuchi Seeds – used as hunting bait to beckon wild animals.

Gotchen – a popular card game that often involves a wager.

Gritbear – a large omnivore with stocky legs and shaggy hair.

Iconel Alloys – materials used to improve durability.

Ilorinae – a territorial plant that can cause fainting spells.

Kamori Powder – pressed ash from the corpse of insects.

Kippin – a type of neutral tea that tastes like water.

Kore – affinity of elemental energy that one is born with.

Larmender – fortified wine made exclusively by House Tepis.

Lucifera Trees – tall and thin tropical trees with wide leaves.

Lorestone – a yellow sharpening stone.

Lumapetal – a herbal plant that grows in wet caves.

Mirithium – a common type of ore used to craft armor.

Muddleberry – a crimson-colored berry used to craft wine.

Norkfruit – a tropical citrus fruit with a purple skin.

Speedspike – plant seeds with a spiky surface.

Swine – a derogatory word used to describe Valenians, who live among nature and are bloated with wealth.

Talla – a symbol or drawing inked into skin.

Valkyrie – Obanian women who become fighters.

Yerna Hay – highly flammable grain crops grown in Valenia.

Zotweed – a mind-altering substance made of dried pedals.

RELIGIONS – It is a common belief that all life departs to either the spiritual world of Nagama or Inferna. If the Gods do not deem the soul worthy to join them in Nagama, they are sent to one of the seven flaming gates of Inferna.

Deity of Orism – Orists believe in one deity: Oris, the God of Judgment. He is primarily worshiped by Althaeans and celtas.

Deities of Quintism – Quintists, common among Minettans, worship only the five main Gods and Goddesses.

Aten – God of Elements
Cordelia – Goddess of War
Sarkan – God of Authority
Taurin – God of Land
Urabe – Goddess of the Sea

Deities of Plethorism – Plethorists acknowledge the existence of hundreds of Gods and Goddesses, but a tribe in Valenia will often choose to praise one or two deities. The following are only a fraction of all known deities:

Accolade – God of Reverence
Candela – Goddess of Purity
Current – God of Negotiation
Cygnus – Goddess of Fate
Erel – Goddess of Mercy
Kanmor – God of Wealth
Lachess – Goddess of Devotion
Mersa – Goddess of Fertility
Mirari – Goddess of Miracles
Ophelia – Goddess of Health
Xerxes – God of Power
Verben – God of Wisdom

Dear Reader,

I am honored that you have made it to this page.

If you enjoyed this read, then please leave
an honest review. Your support
means the world to me.

Love,
Stefanie

Can't wait for the next book? Be the first to
read it when you **become a VIP Member**.
Join today and get free desktop wallpapers.

www.StefanieChu.com/vip

ABOUT THE AUTHOR

 Stefanie is often seen swooning over birds, applying lemon on everything, and torturing herself with bad films. She took advantage of her MBA studies to live in Asia and Europe, and can currently be spotted in her hometown in Northern California.

Learn more at STEFANIECHU.COM

facebook.com/StefanieChu.Author
instagram.com/StefanieChu.Author

THE STORY CONTINUES IN

KNIGHTS OF THE ALLIANCE
Book 1 of the Alliance Series

Fall 2023
Birth of Resilience
Book 2 of the Alliance Series

Summer 2024
Edge of Divergence
Book 3 of the Alliance Series

STEFANIECHU.COM/ALLIANCE